Love,
Life
and
Lust...

Friendship hurts sometimes,
    Friendship cures sometimes...

Love,
Life
and
Lust...

Friendship hurts sometimes,
Friendship cures sometimes...

Pritesh G. Bhosale

Srishti
PUBLISHERS & DISTRIBUTORS

SRISHTI PUBLISHERS & DISTRIBUTORS
N-16, C. R. Park
New Delhi 110 019
srishtipublishers@gmail.com

First published by Srishti Publishers & Distributors in 2012
Copyright © Pritesh G. Bhosale, 2012

All characters in this book are fictitious, and any resemblance to real persons, living or dead, is coincidental.

Typeset in AGaramond 12pt. by Suresh Kumar Sharma at Srishti

Dedicated to all black periods of my life.

Saying thanks

It's not only 14 month's period which is required to complete this story, but it's a dream of more than a decade which made me now a writer of this published book.

A dream which is later on converted to passion and, passion which got wings of words to fly within minds of all.

After lonely traveling in hilly areas of Gujarat and Maharashtra I came to know that I have lot much to say to you all and I must not waste more time for that, and I locked myself in my room at Ahmedabad and there after three days of writing passionately, thirty pages of this story took birth.

But the Novel is never a creation of writer solely there are lots of important peoples who knowingly and unknowingly helped me to travel this journey, The first person appears in my mind is Mr. Kalyan Chowdhary Who sowed seed's of this story in my mind, and as every story this story is also born from true incidences pooled with the fantasy.

Some other truly important person's whom I must say thanks are my brother Vivek, my wife Nivedita for keeping tremendous faith on writer within me, my Aai and Papa.

And Off course Ashwini, Namita, Vipul, Suruchi Raghuvanshi for being the first readers of draft and for believing that there is something good in my writing.

Uday and Gulab (Hope they will not kill me after reading this!).

Also Taher, Ms. Sujata for helping me in cover design, Mr. Ravi palaswadikar, Mr. Ajay Sharma, and Rahim for their efforts in designing cover page and off course Mr. Jayanta kumar Bose and

Srishti editorial team, without them it was impossible to brought this dream into reality.

Thanks to everyone.

Pritesh.

II krishnarpanam II

1
IN AHMEDABAD

It was a cramming day and after my office hours I was going to catch my company bus, I took my mobile phone from company's security cabin where we deposit our mobiles during office hours and I was shocked to see 20 missed calls from Abhi. I caught the bus and then called him with my mind full of silly thoughts.

His phone rang with the same caller tune..babuji jara dheere chalo. "idiot sala nahi sudharega" I muttered to myself.

He picked up the phone and the same vigorous sound came from other side "Hey Mit where were you for eight hours, to hell with your company yaar! Why don't you keep the phone with you?'

"Arey yaar jara saans to le, stop cursing my company buddy and tell me what happened? Why are you calling me like a monster" I replied to him.

"Yaar, who else should I call, listen devil I am getting married and you are the most required person there, come as soon as possible, because my bride will never marry me unless you are there."

"Hey, buddy I can't believe you are going to marry, who is that foolish gal. And for a God's sake ask her once again if she is sure about it?" It was a moment of surprise and shock for me.

"Yes she is damn sure don't worry about that and you know her very well " Abhi continued his series of surprises.

"What! Who is she?"

"She is Priya" Abhi said after a little pause.

"Are you joking? Try something else, it won't work" I was just shocked by listening her name how can he?.......

"I am not at all in the mood for jokes my friend .." now Abhi's voice become serious and firm.

I was so stunned that I couldn't find any words.

"Abhi I can't understand what are you trying to say. I will call you as soon as I reach my room" I spluttered hastily and hanged the phone.

I hung up because it was a deep shock for me and I needed to think over it. A spider of silly thoughts started to spin his web in my mind, can Priya marry Abhi? Surely he is a caring and nice person but after a shock like that .... I don't know. My mind was totally blank.

I went to the room and started to pack my luggage, I wanted to go immediately to Mumbai, and suddenly the phone rang. It was Abhi again, I picked up the phone.

"Hey Mit I know what are you thinking, I will tell you everything but first of all come to Mumbai, and one more thing Priya wants to say something to you. Speak to her" saying this he gave the phone to Priya.

"…hi Mit .." it was Priya's voice and I could hear a slight anxiousness in it, I am worried

She started to speak .. "Mit come here, we both need you.."

"Don't worry Priya I am coming there tomorrow morning. We all will meet at my home" I was talking like the father of a girl.

"We are waiting for you come soon, bye". She said and disconnected the phone.

2
FLASHBACK

I managed to a catch the train for Mumbai somehow, it was 10:30 pm and trying to get a seat in general compartment was useless. So I kept my bag on luggage point and stood at door, holding a door handle.

Cold wind started to strike my face and my mind sprang into the past.

'Past' yeah! In terms of time you can refer it as a past but for me it was always a start, a perfect start of a new era of my life, start of relations which nurtured my soul with their purity and altruism.

I am Maitreya and my gang use to call me Mit. Our so called gang was composed of three pillars Abhi, Dhanu and me, Mit. And as name comes, introduction of these devils becomes necessary....

Abhi a true playboy and an average looking guy but had a great sense of dressing and blessed with a good sense of humor. According to Abhi he immediately knows what a girl really needed, after spending few minutes with her and he honestly tries to be like that only and delivers what she needed, but problem was that he soon got bored with one girl and he changed girlfriends faster than any one of us (and he was always ready to bet over that). I think he continued an affair till he found something challenging in it. His philosophy of love was unbelievable he thought love was nothing but a need of mind and moreover, a need of body.

Me and Dhanu always kept away from his affairs and even he didn't talk about any of his girlfriend when he was with us (except when he was drunk) that's why we were never bothered about his playboy nature, because he was truly nice guy. That's our Abhi.

Abhi's father was a businessman from Satara in Maharashtra, he had a factory of glass bottles manufacturing there, his father had good reputation and also good political connections in that area and most important thing was that he had abundant trust in his son; that's why he sent his son alone in the city like Mumbai to study further as he passed SSC but here, Abhi was like a free bird. There was no one to control him but despite of all the hilarious activities he loved to do always, he maintained a good equilibrium between father's expectations, study and of course girls.

And Dhanu, he was a fair and handsome guy blessed with the height of 6 feet. He had a straight forward nature, Dhanu was from an orthodox family, he was possessive about anything he had.

Dhanu was from Mumbai itself and his mother was a lawyer in a district court and father was working in a state bank so, Dhanu's family was a perfect example of middle class orthodox family living in Mumbai suburbs and as he was only son of his parents, they were little bit possessive about him from his childhood which made Dhanu a little bit self-centered but despite all that Dhanu was a great friend and honest from the bottom of his heart.

And last but not the least, me, I think truly judging yourself is very hard but I think I am a balanced bridge between these two opposite poles. I used to be their court sometimes but true thing was that I was nothing without my friends.

We three were having drastically different opinions about life in my words life is a chance you got to prove yourself, life is a balance of good and bad experiences and your fate is decided upon the behavior you show in your good and bad times.

According to Dhanu life was all about love, relations and sacrifices. You have to love whatever you have, you have to maintain relations with those near you and you must be ready for scarifies for those you love.

And according to Abhi, life is simply lust! But as I know Abhi he did not have lust for anything. He was just enjoying life by his way, and it was his style of living.

It's hard to remember where we first met but our friendship started just because of Mathematics, not because of love for Math but fear of Math, I can remember when I was in 11th and it was our first test of Math and after making a smart rescue from hell of examination hall I entered into a heaven of bunkers called "canteen" and cursing my little pocket money I sat silently drinking water and one healthy boy from my class came to me, sat nearby and said "hey Mit, I have one rupee do you have one we will take a tea half-half".

He was Abhi, I surrendered my one rupee coin to him, hot tea came and our canteen classroom handled several topics related to Math's like why and how to hate Math's? How we don't require this subject at all, how our Math's teacher professor Dhond bores us in class. After that our session decided not to attend lectures of Math's also. After some time Abhi discovered one more boy of our class seating in canteen alone he called him and here I discovered Dhanu, after gathering of we three stooges our luck started sparkling and our conference were discovered by prof. Dhond our Math's professor who came to canteen for having a tea with his colleagues.

Very firstly prof. Dhond discovered Abhi, as a loud and enthusiastic voice of Abhi attracted the ears of prof. Dhond he came a to the place of our conference to see what is going on and he was also delighted to hear some noble thoughts coming from Abhi's mouth in his praise. After a fruitful discussion in canteen with us prof. Dhond invited all of us in his cabin for a reward and the news spread in whole class immediately that we were suspended from mathematics class for next six months. Oh god so kind you are! From then we started to call that day a lucky day in the history of mathematics.

Prof. Dhond was a typical professor of 45 to 47 years age and had a height of 6 feet 3 inches, extraordinarily dark in color, half of his head was covered with hair that seemed to be forcefully colored black and any one could guess easily it was dye as the color could be seen on backside of his neck and his shirt also seemed to take part in this coloring competition.

Prof. Dhond was a historical person as according to him he had participated in numerous rallies, and spent much time in jails in his college days, and we were often blessed with the opportunity of listening to his speeches on his rallies and his jail yatras.

As now we were suspended from his class we missed a lot, the chance of being a part of that journey to the history and to get honored by the heart throbbing names with which Dhond Sir used to call us every time.

Our college days were spent in versatile activities like trying to find perfect girl for Dhanu, trying to sort out various affairs of Abhi, trying to escape from Dhond Sir's eyes. Trying to spend maximum time in canteen and least time in class. So many things were there which we learned together like – smoking cigarette. Abhi learned to make rings of smoke and always used to do that to make us feel jealous.

But besides that we learned to study in groups because it became necessary when you had to do the one night show. One night show was the name given by us to the study sessions one night before exams, as in between all these busy activities it became very hard for us to find the time to study so the night before the exam was always a judgment night for us.

We always used to kidnap Ramesh, a nerd from our class and favorite student of Prof. Dhond. One night before the exams, and the place of the session was my room which was on the first floor of my home. And that night used to be sleepless for us especially for Ramesh as he had to teach three of us from scratch whatever subject that was to be tested the next day as well as study for himself.

3
THE OATH

It was the day before our final results of HSC. In the morning at 8 my phone rang, I picked up and it was Abhi's usual voice "hey, Mit where are you, you devil?"

Devil was his favorite word to start or end any conversation. I tried many times to tell him to improve his way of speaking but he was Abhi and we always used to say "Abhi will never change". So it was useless to tell him anything.

Abhi's voice was frustrated, so I replied to him "I am sleeping yaar"

"You bloody monster how can you sleep, tomorrow is our result day" his voice become more frustrated.

"So what? Did you give a thought to this day in the whole year? Nahi na… then why to take tension at the eleventh hour? Just chill and let me sleep, I explained to him my great philosophy.

But Abhi was Abhi, so he came to my home with his Yamaha and started blowing the horn like a monster; I went out and yelled with a voice louder than his horn "Abey gadhe, come in otherwise my neighbors will kill you".

He came in with the face like someone is about to kill him and he somehow made an escape and came to me! I offered him a seat while I was still in the bed.

"Get up! You devil, look at me; my head is about to burst thinking of the results and you are still in bed, enjoying day dreaming" He shouted while shaking my body vigorously.

"Calm down you desperate pig and let me get fresh. We will go out"

I quickly brushed up and changed cloths and got ready to go out. Abhi was like this only, he was spontaneous, he got excited, frustrated or desperate easily.

We directly went to the Dhanu's house. After picking up Dhanu our next spot was definitely the college ground where there was our reserved corner where we used to sit every evening and we used to call it "a college katta"

"You know what is the time right now bloody full, its morning 10:30 and you called us to smoke with you on this ground are you gone mad?" Dhanu shouted on Abhi with cigarette in one hand, and stared at my face for response, but I kept quite.

"What would I do yaar, I am scared for the results" Abhi answered.

"Okay, I was also worried for our results because I know what we did for the whole year but then what I can do if there is nothing in my hands than waiting?" Dhanu is talking like a professor.

"The best we can do is just keep ourselves calm and watch" I added.

"I have a plan .." its Abhi opening an idiot box of his mind once again.

"We will celebrate today itself, we don't know what's there for us in tomorrow, scene might be like that all are celebrating and we are staring them with the sick faces, so why not to enjoy at this moment only, lets go to Anna's bar friends" Abhi's eyes are now looking like a two year kid who finds something very interesting to play with.

"Oh! Monster then this is your plan for this only you dragged me out of bed at 8:00" I opened my mouth after situation was clear to me.

"This silly fellow is creating one more crisis for us" now it's turn of Dhanu.

"Listen me guys please…." Abhi tried to clear his side.

But there was no need as I and Dhanu started bike and Dhanu said

"Okay, lets go to hell together after all how can we let you go alone there."

And we finally landed at Anna's bar. It was a typical Dhaba on the highway, at some distance from the city. The Dhaba was quite old as was visible from its walls. The ceiling was of slim steel and one old fan was revolving with a huge effort.

The dhaba owner, Anna, saw us and he loudly called Abhi whom he seemed to know very well.

"What happened? This is a time to drink milk, go home and drink milk. Dhaba is closed".

"Anna, today we need Madeira not the milk, we don't know your timings but you have to do this for us for today" Abhi replied to Anna in a funny voice.

"Abhi, I think you might be having credit account here" Dhanu asked Abhi while looking at the jar.

"No yaar, one of my friend knows Anna very well." Abhi answered.

"And that creature must be Gulab" Dhanu chuckled.

"I think you are a regular here! Don't worry we will never mind, I have just one query, why haven't you shown us this place before". I was trying to pull Abhi's leg but he just laughed in reply and called Golu for taking order.

"Golu, one chilled beer, two packet peanuts fast.." Abhi ordered and moved towards our faces 'anything else guys'.

"No, Gurudev as you wish after all you always knows what's there in our mind so, what's the need for us to speak" now it was Dhanu's turn to pulling his leg. And Abhi had again no choice but ignore it, he was just eager to let that chilled beer go down his throat.

Finally the bottle came and the opener in the Golu's hands done his work and the great smell came out of it which started doing magic on our minds.

"So guys now forget everything and just enjoy the moment" Abhi announced the start of the party by raising his glass high, a toast was made and finally beer made a successful attempt in reaching its destination.

Party started and countdown of bottles also began.

We started at around 11:00 and now was 3:30, countdown of bottles now reached at 6, Dhanu and I declared our innings and relaxed in the chairs. And now it time for Abhi to start his mouth factory.

"You know guys what brought us here?" Abhi started his second inning and we both were the unfortunate victims.

"Your bike". I bantered.

"No, man it's the system! It's our bloody system which frustrated us in such a way that we were forced to drink this bloody alcohol. Tell me my friends; tell me from the bottom of your heart what are we? Are we students? Or we are living a life like a cockroach? What did you think, I say we are nothing but cockroaches no.. Sorry cockroaches have a better life than us because for the entire year we think of books, exams and score! That's all and what is our achievement at the end? Just a mark sheet which will just help us in getting admission to another course or getting a job to earn money that's it! Is this life? No friends, we have something in us which we have to develop and we have to break the system together". Abhi finished his short speech with both hands in the air and eyes towards us.

Suddenly sound of clapping came from the corner we all looked behind it was golu, "Wah sir! You can be a good politician". Golu gave his response to Abhi's great speech which was actually an impact of the sixth recently finished bottle.

"Fuck you all, bloody fools if you don't believe in a system then, why are you studying and why you are scared of your fucking result, you know what? You are behaving like a hypocrite" now it was Dhanu's turn, I knew that this was going to happen. How will he keep quite after all, he has also contributed in finishing six bottles.

"Both of you fuckers keep quiet and stop this nonsensical fight, yaar! concentrate on the situation, unless and until we get good qualification how can we change the system? Unfortunately for changing the system we have to be a part of this system but despite of being part of the system we have to keep our mind clean and selfless" and thus I also entered into fuckers fight but fortunately I found a middle point of their fight before they were at each other's throat and thank almighty that both agreed on that.

And now the time came to take a final oath Abhi stood on the chair which fortunately handled his weight somehow after fluctuating twice. Taking care of his body weight Abhi raised the hand to take the final oath.

"Dear friends hear on 12th march 2001 today on 4:00 pm I Abhishek Patil also representing Mr. Maitreya and Mr. Dhananjay takes an oath that we will never let down the fire burnt in our hearts today, we all will stand united, fight united and this is our promise to the generation to come that we will never let them suffer through this system we will definitely give them the new world to take breath".

Thus the Anna's classroom ended with the mutual agreement between three of us.

4
JUDJEMENT DAY

Rays of sun fell on my eyes in the morning and I discovered myself in Abhi's room, Dhanu and Abhi were sleeping over each other, I looked at my watch, oh! No it was 9:00 and today was our results day, mom would be worried I thought and tried to wake Dhanu up to go home.

"Hey Dhanu, wake up yaar we have to go to the college! Today is our results day we also haven't informed at our home" my voice sounded flustered.

Dhanu slightly opened his eyes and said, "I already have informed at your and my home at night, so chill we will go to college directly from here".

"Okay, thanks for that then awake this elephant first" I said quite relaxing.

A better comparison for Abhi's ramshackle and shattered room I ever found was nothing but a Railway Platform because at railway platform there are lots of passengers spending their time for few hours to sometime a day and nobody knows each other. Abhi's room was stuff like that, where everything like news papers, his books, clothes were scattered all over the room in such a manner that things could not be found easily, to search anything one had to be very familiar with the room like Abhi or one had be a James Bond, Abhi never knows how many people stayed in his room with him, he practically had to see faces of peoples lying on the floor every night when he came in the room because most of faces vanished in morning before he got up and every time he discovered at least one new face in his room. Sometimes he got his introduction and sometimes not, thanks to the another adventurous animal staying in Abhi's room. "Gulab" as the name indicates, Gulab was a really Great and hilarious creature of god. He was four years older than us and studying Engineering, Third year. Gulab was sharing Abhi's room because of Abhi's fathers instructions, as he was from their native place and Abhi's family had good relations with his family. Gulab was a good looking guy but not like a prince charming about who every girl fantasizes about, he was okay with whatever he was but had lots of misconceptions about himself. Gulab was an amazing freak having no relation with the world and nor ever interested in what's going around him, his attendance in college totally depends on his mood. One could easily identify him by his black lips, thanks to the cigarettes. He smoked every single minute, his fat floppy, spongy tummy thanks to the bottles of beer he used to drink every night at Anna's Dhaba, and his slouching gait.

The reason behind this condition of Gulab is his so called breakup with a girl whom he met in Pune while studying in Diploma Engineering.

He had a very good relation with that girl even both families were aware of their relation but despite that, suddenly the girl's marriage was fixed with a good looking NRI guy. And girl started to avoid Gulab, as she suddenly found him not so good looking.

Whatever it may be but after that Gulab's life became shoddier and there was no one to understand him and even now he did not want anyone to interfere in his life he wanted to live by his own rules now but Abhi and his room became poor victim of all this as he had to deal with his drinking partners coming every night to sleep in his rooms after their soul has gone to the ride on seventh cloud.

Actually Abhi's stayed in a bungalow purchased by Abhi's father. He purchased this bungalow as soon as his son got admission in this city because he wanted his son to concentrate on studies and he thought that Abhi will have more privacy for studying if he had his own place rather than living in a shared room.

And as his thinking his son was really enjoying his private life and now going to face the fruits of his so called hard work throughout the year.

After getting fresh we started our march towards kaki's canteen.

Kaki is the canteen owner and she had a canteen for tea and breakfast near by Abhi's room.

We ordered tea while sitting on the benches at canteen and I saw Ramesh coming towards us with a smiley face, I signaled Abhi and Dhanu to see.

I know this Dracula always smiles at a wrong time and this time his smile might be an indication of something very dangerous. My heart started beating fast.

"Come devil" Abhi welcomed him in his patented way and offered a tea.

"No time for tea guys, I have a copy of results downloaded from the internet. Tell me your seat nos. fast. I will check whether you have passed or failed" Ramesh said in his innocent way.

"Go away you fool, you will never let us live with peace" Abhi shouted on him suddenly very angrily and withdrawn his cup of tea offered to him.

"Okay, yaar let him settle down and sit properly" I interfered in between.

"Yaar, result has already been announced and we have to face it some time or the other so why not now. Ramesh check the results these are our seat nos. written on this page". I took charge of the moment and gave him a chit.

Ramesh started finding seat nos. and we all were looking at his face, that seen is really photogenic but we were unaware that we are looking so stupid.

'Found!' Ramesh shouted with excitement just like he had found any diamond in stones.

"Whose number?" Abhi asked silently.

"Its Dhanu, and he is ....pass!"

'Yes!' Dhanu jumped in excitement. And Abhi and my face became more anxious.

"Ramesh see my no. is it there?" Now Abhi was helpless and left his resistance for seeing results.

"Your is ....yes! Abhi has passed"

Abhi jumped like a kid and the moment brought a childish smile on his face.

Now remained me ....again a silence.

"Yes! Mit is also passed."

And finally tension was converted to joy, sorrow was transferred to happiness, we did not have eagerness of seeing how marks we secured, we neither having interests in class we achieved or our rankings, we are happy to know that we had passed our HSC that's it!.

Taking admissions to your favorite stream was more difficult and hectic than qualifying the board exams, and we soon realized that.

As was obvious, three of us did not secure sufficient marks to get admissions easily to any stream and tried each and every stream as per well known funda 'beggars can't be choosers'.

Finally, I got the admissions to Pharmacy thanks to my father for choosing Army as his carrier because I got admission under Army quota.

After much effort Dhanu got admissions to Computer science and Abhi got admissions in engineering thanks to his father for selecting business as his career as he got admission on a paid seat.

Our careers got separated but our souls couldn't be separated at any cost our routine remained undisturbed, thanks to almighty god that our college campus was almost same so our habit of remaining with each other did not change, just our colleges changed, classrooms remained same - college canteen.

5
LOVE IS IN THE AIR

I will never forget that day of my life. It was 6th Jan 2002, when we planned to go for a movie. Me and Abhi were waiting for Dhanu to come, we were getting late for the show and Dhanu was still missing, Abhi tried on his cell but no use. He was not picking the phone so, while cursing him we decided to move on and suddenly we heard Dhanu's bikes and,

"Oh there comes the devil" Abhi said.

We moved to call him and to tell him to come fast but the next moment both of us stood shocked there was a beautiful and decent girl with him, she was fair in color and looking great in the blue salwar kameez, her curly hairs were rolling over her cheeks. She was looking very confident.

The first thing I did after watching her was to shut the open mouth of Abhi, and welcomed both of them with smile, they were moving towards us and I could notice a childish smile on Dhanu's face and for sure it was marvelous.

Dhanu started her introduction "Mit, Abhi she is Priya she is my classmate. We are good friends and she wanted to meet both of you so, I planned to bring her for the movie"

Hi! Both of us greeted her in one voice.

"I am so sorry boys actually I have heard so much about both of you and wanted to meet you so I couldn't just stop myself from coming here, and it was my plan to give you a surprise visit. So sorry for being late". Girl tried to explain her side.

"Oh! No way we are not at all angry it was a nice surprise, we will talk to our 'chupa rustum' some other time" Abhi tried to be a nice guy.

"We are very glad to meet you Priya but just surprised that our friend hadn't told us about you, and it was really a great idea to join us" and it was my turn.

We followed them to the cinema hall, Abhi whispered into my ears "Hey, Mit what did you think Dhanu's having an affair and didn't ever talk to us about that".

"Shut your mouth Abhi! It will be discussed later on" I warned him and he just nodded.

After the movie we halt at our "college katta" which is near the cinema hall. It was 11:30 pm.

"Yeah Priya I think you might be knowing sufficient stuff about us so tell us something about you" I tried to break the ice.

'Yeah she is from...' Dhanu started to be her advocate but Abhi interrupted him

"Let her speak Dhanu, she is old enough to tell about herself"

"Okay, I am from Pune, my parents are doctor and I am staying here in the college hostel".

Our chat lasted for an hour after that Dhanu dropped her to hostel and we separated and that night we discovered a fourth pillar of our gang 'Priya'.

No wonder that Priya very soon become a vital part of our group in other words in just a month she became a thread that kept three of us more bounded.

Now she was our organizer cum advisor for every meeting or event and we became addicted of her presence every time.

now our group has a girl so it become necessary to behave like a gentleman and by god we tried our best to be like that but no use habits cant be changed and after all guys are guys. Thanks to Priya who was a cool, modern girl and she adjusted very well with us now we could talk about Abhi's latest affairs with her and also she started to search a cool girl for me. She was really a lovely friend.

Abhi and I started to notice Dhanu's feelings for her. He was a true caring person by heart but this time it was more than just care. He was involved in her and as friends, it was our turn to play our role in this love story and we did that.

Abhi and I decided to do something that will bring Dhanu and Priya closer and Abhi's idiot box brought a brand new idea, a picnic on the occasion of Abhi's birthday which was very near, yah! It was Abhi's real birthday on 24th feb, actually this Dracula was having another story of his so called birthdays. Abhi celebrates his birthday twice a year one is real and one official, real birthday is a date on which he actually appeared on earth and official is one which is used by him officially on certificates to make others full, I heard from his mother that when he was child he used to harass her always by his so called versatile activities so to get rid of such energetic activities of this uncommon child she admitted him in a school by showing him one year elder than he actually was with a fake birth date, and being a genuine person Abhi also used to celebrate both of these days as his birthday.

And as friends we always supported his enormous philosophies so why not this after all we are the people who were directly getting benefits of it.

So date is fixed venue is also decided Abhi did all the stuff to make his birthday party successful venue was 'Matheran' which is a hill station in Neral near to Mumbai we used to go their by local train and from neral to matheran by mini train thanx to Abhi that he booked tickets so early.

We reached at the destination environment was really cool, nice cold wind was flowing, touching body and healing the soul, all the burden of mind was just vanished and soul entered in the another new world, for a new aspirant of love this was an ideal time where nature was supporting them and I think if any girl says no to boy who she likes in this atmosphere then she might be dumb.

Abhi jumped from the as it stopped, and started running may be he immediately wanted to go away from these love birds to give them some space or he had seen some girl over there and didn't wanted to miss the chance to get her intro, any ways I had to follow this asshole,

So, I ran behind him, it was a kuccha road made by people's feet. We started to run towards a echo point, a red soil started to assault my clothes. It was a sign of konkan a red soil, and greenery every where you see, that's why konkan is said to be southern Kashmir.

Abhi stopped at one spot so did I, "hey monkey have you gone mad running like a mental who has recently escaped from a hospital", I shouted.

"You will never understand Mit let them have their own time yaar" Abhi explained his philosophy while bending his body in different angles and trying to take more oxygen to settle.

"But yaar we have to talk with Dhanu firstly we have to encourage him we didn't know whether he will propose her or not?" I expressed my worry.

"I think you are right yaar, we have to talk to him otherwise he will just waste this day" Abhi proved that he is a tube light.

We just turned back and we are stunned to see the scene Dhanu and Priya were walking together and have goofed hands.

"I think we are stupid look at that" I said while eyes stuck on them.

"Yeah friend but we have to check it with Dhanu whether they are talking of point or not even realized that there hands were goofed"

Abhi called Dhanu with loud voice and suddenly he aroused like he was walking in dream and pulled his hand back.

"I think you are right Abhi this guy is really a donkey" I said.

We went towards them, Priya smiled looking at us like she had not met us in a day, and smiling to say hi!

"Hey Priya you please just wait for us for a while we will come by purchasing something to eat you can seat on that bench" said Abhi by pointing towards a bench at corner.

Priya nodded, and we dragged Dhanu with us towards a snacks stall.

Abhi dragged Dhanu at a corner of stall hold his arms tightly and started his loveguru style class,

"You monkey, what you thought we planned this picnic for the sake of my birthday only.

Or just to pass a time on this hill talking on pollution and traffic problems of city".

"Then what will I do, I can't dare more than this yaar" Dhanu outburst his feelings with little frustration.

"Be a man!, we know that she loves you and she is waiting for a proposal from your side. Be bold yaar" Abhi now become aggressive to taught his philosophy.

Okay….. but what if she rejected me then what will happen with our friendship?" Dhanu was still confused.

Now I took charge, and said

"Look Dhanu this hesitation is okay but don't you think that you are cheating her by hiding your emotions from her".

"Yeah I think you are right yaar, I should say sorry to her first" Dhanu changed the track totally

Now Abhi, losing his patience, became more aggressive and held Dhanu's shoulders more tightly and said "listen today will be your judgment day. Either you are going to tell her or I am going to take this responsibility".

"Okay, guys I understand. I will propose her today but please give me some time to gather the courage" Dhanu surrendered to us and now Abhi's eyes sparkled.

"Okay, take this hot coffee cup and go to her. You have lots of time, don't worry we are waiting here and send me a message as you succeed in this mission" I pushed him towards the place where she was waiting by giving two coffee cups in his hands.

Dhanu just nodded and left the place.

We purchased two hot coffees and cream rolls to pass time. About 45 minutes passed after Dhanu left us and since then there was no ring nor a message from him, we both were eager to know the situation.

"Definitely this fool has created some dilemma I am sure something is wrong there" Abhi was disturbed and I acted like I hadn't heard anything.

Suddenly Abhi's phone beeped it was Dhanu's message and Abhi shouted as he seen that "Hey Mit here he is!"

"Read it then yaar fast"

Message was "cum soon! Big crisis".

"Oh no!" Abhi reacted with frustration suddenly as he read the message.

"Let's go Abhi we have to solve this, after all we are responsible. We pushed him into this dilemma" I kept my coffee cup aside and stood up to go towards Dhanu and Priya, Abhi followed me with no argument now.

We went near the bench where they were sat, they were sitting at the opposite ends of the bench keeping large distance between each other, Priya was hiding her face with her palms and she seemed to be crying.

We stood in front of her like prisoners of war and I initiated silently "Priya we are really very sorry, we didn't mean that. Actually, it was really our mistake we forced Dhanu and for that we are really sorry.

Priya please forgive us…."

There was no reply from Priya's side hands still hiding the face so I bent on knees and tried to see her face.

Suddenly she removed her palms from face and started to laugh vigorously.

"What's this yaar!" It was a shock we both were shocked and at the other end Dhanu also started to laugh.

"Disgusting! Guys you both are playing with us?" Abhi reacted with anger.

"I am really sorry guys, this was Priya's idea" Dhanu

"Really sorry, I just wanted to see your faces and its really awesome, and after all you all started this", Priya reacted by taking a pause from laugh.

"Okay, forget all this! tell us what happen what's the result of all this stuff" I eagerly asked about the proposal.

"Chill Mit I will tell you everything in tonight's party" Dhanu said, holding my shoulder,

And this time his eyes were speaking more than him, so one needed no clue to understand what happened to his proposal.

Abhi's tube light sparked and he jumped with a joy "Hey that means yes! Priya said yes! Yeah look you fool I was telling you nah! I never guide anyone in the wrong direction."

"Yes Gurudev, it's because of you only I could never show her my feelings, thank you! Guys you are real friends" Dhanu became emotional and hugged both of us.

Priya was looking to us and she sees to be emotional by watching this Hindi film style friendship she interrupted us " hey guys we can show more 'mitraprem' later on, right now I am too much hungry is there any my true friend to take my care?".

Abhi jumped to Priya's side and said "Hey Priya don't worry Abhi is always there for you, and if this fool tortures you in future, don't forget to call me at any time. After all a friend in need is a friend in deed so, lets go to the food..".

They moved towards a hotel for lunch and we followed them. It was happy ending to the day with a nice treat, and after that a day started to pack up his special box, also sun was in a hurry to rise in another part of the world and we were returning back to Mumbai.

Abhi dropped Priya to her hostel at 8:00 pm on his bike and Dhanu and I preferred to wait at 'college katta'.

"Dhanu, Priya was looking very happy today, and I am sure you will keep her like this only" I started to speak, lighting my cigarette.

"Yeah Mit she is really a cute girl and I think I am very lucky to have her and both of you in my life" Dhanu was getting emotional as his hand moved to pick a cigarette and I suddenly hit on his hand.

"hey, you should leave smoking now, Priya doesn't like it" I said taking cigarette packet away from him.

"Oh now you are killing me emotionally yaar" Dhanu cried like a child.

"This is life, my friend, be trained of it after all our packet will live longer now, how could we let this chance go" I bantered.

Abhi came with identical bike sound.. "hey guys you know Priya is very happy even she promised me to introduce to that Puja".

"Oh! You mean that giraffe, you know that she is one feet taller than you" I expressed my view.

"Then what yaar, love sees nothing only heart should sound same. Love is blind guys and now she is love of the month" Abhi expressed his view.

"Oh! You bloody fucker! You will never ever change and please don't ever tell Priya this nonsense philosophy she will definitely kick you" we started to laugh at him.

And that night was called with half dozen cigarettes and dozens of smiles.

6
ROMANCE AND CHAOS

Academic year came to its end and off course brought lots of tensions and frustrations with it and off course it's a tough time for the emotional fools like us.

Although now we had different fields and different syllabus for study but our exams were scheduled near about in a same period and our exam preparation leaves started so we gathered at Abhi's room and it was our first day of PL . Ramesh's space was now filled by Priya but the difference was that I was studying Pharmacy, Abhi was studying engineering and Priya, Dhanu had to study computer science.

I came from home to study at Abhi's room at 12:30 and that donkey was still sleeping, door was open and news papers were scattered all over in the room. Broken cigarettes and ashes also had covered some places of the room like windows, all corners and near the bed. I became anxious by watching the scene and I kicked his butt very hard to wake him up as this is the only validated way to wake him.

"hey, Mit let me sleep for some time yaar" Abhi whispered by drawing his blanket over his head.

"Wake up you asshole how can you do this yaar? You are the person who invites all of us even Priya to study in this bloody shattered devils den and you are the person who sleeps until sun comes on the head with these bloody cigarettes scattered all over the room. You are really unstoppable yaar I don't know what to do with you" I expunged all my frustration and waited for the result.

That devil slightly withdrew his blanket and stared around and made facial expression like he has seen any horrifying scene from a Hollywood film.

"Oh no, I am so sorry yaar I forgot everything, I was listening to Britney till 1:00 at night. I really forgot this" Abhi said while getting out of the bed.

"Time hasn't gone still we have to clean the room before Priya comes" I said initiating collection of news papers scattered in the room.

"Hey, and where's that creature called 'Gulab' I wondered there is no one in your room" I asked while cleaning the room.

"He went to home his father called him there is some problem like court case related to their land so he went to help his father"

Abhi answered.

My phone rang and it was Dhanu, I picked the phone Dhanu told that he and Priya are on their way to Abhi's room.

"Hey Abhi come on get ready they are coming" I give him a call he was in the bath room to get ready I cleaned the room and after some minutes they came.

"Hi! Mit I thought you both has started studying" Priya said while removing her sandals.

"Oh! How could you expect this from us yaar you will get to know today only how we study and how serious we are about the exams" I cleared her misunderstanding about us after all there should not be the place for misunderstanding in the friendship.

Yaar Priya every one can clear the exams after studying hard but the real gems are those who pass without study. Don't you agree?" Abhi contributed from the bathroom.

"Yeah, Abhi is always right" Priya laughed and sat on the bed.

"Hey Priya are you going to start study immediately?" Dhanu questioned like she was breaking some bible rule made by god himself.

"Yes, so what? Is there something wrong?" Priya was surprised.

"Yeah! We mean we are not habitual of starting study immediately you know we can't concentrate so early yaar we have to discuss some general topics you know just like athlete takes a warm up before taking a part in the competition" Abhi while getting out of the bathroom he has to contribute as he is a excuse king of us.

"Yeah! I understood all your excuses. Now you have to change your habits! Do whatever you want to do in 5 minutes and gather here for studying".

Now, Priya was taking a charge of us and thought it necessary because there should be at least one reasonable person among a gang of all careless freaks to give us a right direction and a girl fits correctly in that role. After all, who would deny anything to Priya? At least I will not for sure.

Abhi came quickly like a good boy, Dhanu was quite. He was taking a chance of staring at her and seemed to be busy in that. He settled himself in one corner.

"Hey, let's have a tea first we can start our study with a new energy haa?" Abhi said.

Priya agreed and we ordered tea from Kaki's canteen at the room itself.

Tea came and I, suddenly remembered Puja, Abhi's love of the month "Hey Abhi you hadn't told us about that Puja, did Priya introduced you to her".

Priya laughed suddenly as she heard about Puja and Abhi's face become mortified.

"Leave it yaar she is one feet taller than me" Abhi replied and now Dhanu also started laughing.

"You scoundrel, were we telling you this in Chinese at that time, what were you telling us 'oh friends Love is blind blah.. blah.. blah...'

what about that nonsense love of the month, we were telling you nah that she doesn't suit you" I totally used the moment to embarrass him again.

"Yes yaar but she told me the same thing and you knows better I respect every girls feelings" Abhi replied.

"You rascal" Dhanu yelled at him and threw a pillow at him. I also joined him by attacking Abhi with books kept on my side.

Environment become funny rather than serious about exams it took two hours to settle us down and concentrate on studying thanks to Priya. I think she will be a good mother after all she proved it by handling dangerous kids like us, what will be worse than this?.

Abhi sat in one corner, I choose a chair to sit and Dhanu and Priya were studying together sitting on the mattress. Abhi was observing Dhanu. He was trying his hardest to concentrate on what Priya was teaching him but poor fellow, his eyes were telling everything. He was taking every chance to stare Priya, there are lot more things going in his mind except study and it seems to be like he wanted to share some time privately with her but couldn't speak anything because of our presence and our Gurudev Mr. Abhishek Patil identified this dilemma very well.

One hour passed and Abhi's expiry date for studying came on its edge so, he attracted my concentration by throwing a paper ball and gestured me to come outside I followed him as I have no any other way to escape.

"Hey did you notice that fool how desperately he was looking at her?" Abhi started in his patented way.

"Yeah I have noticed it but then what's wrong in it? They love each other and it is human nature to get attracted towards opposite sex" I explained to him, the depth of human psychology.

"Mit don't teach me that bookish stuff yaar. Try to understand what I want to say yaar!"

"Okay, speak up"

"Did you think that this fellow has done anything yet?"

"Anything? What's that?"

"Anything means not just anything yaar it means the thing which is necessary to express love"

"Yeah, he had proposed her and he takes good care of her"

"Oh! God next time give me at least intelligent friends" Abhi yelled with frustration.

"okay I am talking about a kiss! A simple kiss which I think is a necessary means of expressing a love and without it love is incomplete" Abhi was now talking like our English Professor of HSC who is in our opinion responsible for so many affairs in our college pupils influenced by his lectures tried to do the practical of love and finally left it cursing him but his only successful student is Abhi and as a obedient student of him Abhi will now teach his own lessons of love to the world.

"Look Abhi don't try to interfere in their personal matter. Dhanu is a mature guy he knows what he has to do" I tried to control Abhi's emotions by saying this but I knew that it was useless.

"Oh, I am not interfering in any personal matter yaar! I just want my friends love life happy and I know that it won't be without my help"

"Okay, if you have decided not to listen to me then do whatever you want to do"

"Don't get angered yaar Mit! We will just have a talk with Dhanu and believe me we are just helping him to express his own emotions, you just wait! I will call him" Abhi called Dhanu by some silly excuse and we went outside the gate of the bungalow.

"Dhanu what did you think we hadn't noticed what you were doing for an hour now" Abhi started his one more motivational speech.

"Hey what are you talking about yaar? I didn't do anything!" Dhanu was confused totally by Abhi's bouncer.

"That's what I want to say you didn't do anything yet, yaar shame on you, you have proposed to a beautiful girl of your college, she said yes to you and she is spending much of her day's time with you and you don't realize your responsibility" Dhanu wasn't stabilized from last bouncer and one more came.

"I didn't understand you yaar what did you want to say please elaborate it" Dhanu

"I will simplify it for you. Just answer me. You are having an affair with Priya for the last two-three months. Did you ask her for a date?"

"Date?...No" Dhanu answered first Question.

"Okay then did you have a romantic chat with her when both of you were alone with sun calling for his day at seashore?" second googly

No. Dhanu again played defensively.

"Then did you kiss her at least, my friend?"

"No way yaar" now Dhanu is stumped.

"You know my friend there are two types of communications in love one is verbal communication and other is by touch and sorry to say my friend you are losing on both the fronts" now Abhi was on the high.

"Okay yaar I wanted to go close to her but I am afraid what she will think of me and all that"

"I am telling you that go and kiss her, I am saying that fill your relation with romance because it's an essential part of your relation talk with her without any reason that will take both of you more closer not that C++ or java".

"Okay then tell me what to do now"

"Okay, for the time being concentrate on study and in evening when you are going to drop her at hostels take her to the 'college katta' no one will be there after 8:00"

"And then?"

"Talk romantic yaar"

"Okay ..okay I will try, yaar actually I was thinking about a date but was afraid to ask because of exams but this is quite good idea we can have a chat over there" Dhanu was seems to be quite stable and happy now.

After this session we went to study and tried hard to concentrate but to expect more in first day is injustice with you, so we honestly passed most of the time in tea and nashta at kaki's canteen.

At evening Dhanu left us to drop Priya and we said goodbye with high hopes.

Dhanu turned his bike to college katta and stopped.

"What happened Dhanu?" Priya asked.

"We have studied for a day yaar lets have some relaxing moments"

"Relax? we already have relaxed a lot Dhanu! Lets go"

"Oh, I am not talking about just relaxing I am talking about some romantic moments, have we ever talked on any needless subject or any subject not related to studies, college etcetera".

"Oh… you want to be romantic now"

"Yeah, absolutely"

"Okay then you have 10 minutes! Go ahead"

"Hey, don't be so rude yaar"

"Dhanu, I don't know how to be romantic so, I am sorry I can't help you"

"What do you mean yaar, and then I knew it? Okay leave it, tell me do you love me?"

"Don't ask silly questions" says Priya and stood up for leaving the place Dhanu held her hand and she suddenly stopped as if she was just acting to go and wanted some force from Dhanu's side to stop her.

"Hey tell me nah" Dhanu pulled her towards him by saying this.

"I think you are getting naughty"

"Oh, I am naughty! And what you are doing, is that justice?"

"Priya do you love me?"

"Is it necessary to prove it?"

"Yes, it is" now Dhanu cupped her face with both of his hands and she suddenly became silent she was just frozen at the moment only sound of breaths followed by heartbeats could be heard loudly, Dhanu took his face more closer to her and kissed on her cheeks, she couldn't understood what was going on, until his warm lips touched her cheek and suddenly she withdrew herself from his hold and moved away from him Dhanu was the most embarrassed person on the earth, Dhanu talked to himself in frustration "oh god what have I done! shit...."

"Lets go Dhanu" Priya said in a low voice.

Dhanu sat on the bike and started it immediately dropped her to the hostel but both didn't speak a word to each other.

Later on at midnight my phone rang Dhanu was on the other side.

"hey Mit I am in a big dilemma yaar. I think she misunderstood me"

"What happened? Did you say something wrong to?"

"Nothing like that yaar, but I did something wrong"

"What?"

"I kissed her, and after that she didn't say anything".

Dhanu told me everything, and I understood the dilemma.

"Hey! there is nothing to worry about my friend, its common in new relationships".

"What's common yaar? Everything went wrong! What would she be thinking about me? I am gone my friend I have lost her"

"Hey, there is nothing like that buddy! You haven't lost her, listen to me carefully! She will think of only you for a whole night and will definitely call you in the morning. After her call go and meet her, everything will be clear after that" I tried to calm down Dhanu .

And it happened as per my guess Priya called Dhanu at sharp 9:00 to come and collect her to go to the Abhi's place he went to her but both of them didn't talk to each other and here I told Abhi to disappear from the room just before they came to the room. So I and Abhi hid our selves at Kakis canteen and here Dhanu and Priya came and surprised to see door of the room opened with nobody inside Dhanu tried on my and Abhi's nos. but no use, mine was switched off and Abhi's in the room itself.

"Let's get to study Dhanu, they must have gone for breakfast" Priya said while sitting on the mattress.

Dhanu sat down silently. Some time passed and Dhanu started to become impatient, he came to the Priya and sat beside her.

"I am so sorry Priya, I didn't want to hurt you. I was just wanted to express my love"

Priya turned around, she seems to be emotionless

"I know Dhanu, am I talking about that incidence?"

"But you are not talking to me na! Please forgive me"

Dhanu held Priya's hand and started to cry and plead for forgiveness and seeing that he was totally disturbed from inside, Priya held Dhanu's face and pulled him closer to her.

"Dhanu there is no need to feel guilty and I know someday we will pass this phase, so please don't cry"

Dhanu's face became somewhat happy and relaxed on hearing this from her.

And next moment Priya placed her head on Dhanu's shoulders, to show him that she felt secure with him.

Dhanu's right hand was moving back and forth on Priya's back to make her feel comfortable.

After some time she moved slightly upward. Dhanu was now holding her tightly pulled her towards him and put his lips on her neck and started kissing, now Priya became inert and closed her eyes. Her silence was like permission to Dhanu for letting happen whatever was happening. Now Dhanu put his lips on Priya's lips and they started smooching. Dhanu's hands started moving on hilly areas of Priya's body, Dhanu's hands started opening buttons of her kurti, Priya laid on Dhanu's body now, and became slightly active her hands were moving on Dhanu's face hairs, Dhanu pulled her bra and turned himself on top by landing her body on mat Dhanu removed his shirt now Priya hugged Dhanu tightly their bodies melt in each other. Lying in the same position Priya opened her eyes cupped Dhanu's face with her hands and said

"I love you Dhanu, I am only yours, Dhanu don't ever think that I will be with annoyed you"

"I love you too Priya, I will never hurt you" says Dhanu

Priyas eyes become moist Dhanu wiped her tears with his lips and kissed her cheeks

"Hey baby, are you crying? We will not cross our limits beta" says Dhanu while moving his hand on Priya hairs.

"it's not like that Dhanu don't mind it's just natural I think we should stop here." Said Priya while pulling back her hand from Dhanu's body.

Both become separate and laid their bodies aside and remained in the same position for some time. The pair didn't crossed their limits may be because they wanted to give some more time to their relation to become mature or may be because it was too early in the new relation to get physical as per Priya's way of thinking but Priya crossed her limits just to show Dhanu that how much she loved him and she could not just see him crying she fulfilled his desire of kiss with more than he expected. It's not about getting physical in the relation, it's a way to express someone's love and care for the one he loves more than anything.

Dhanu now has understood that thing; love doesn't need the aid of words to express itself. Love is feeling which could be felt through touch, which could be sensed through smell, Love is a business of two hearts which doesn't needs at all the help of fundamental things of the practical world.

After some time Priya wore her cloths and went for getting fresh. Dhanu also dressed up

"Wanna have coffee? Let's go to the canteen" Dhanu asked

"Yes, let's go" Priya answered.

Abhi and me were just passing time by smoking cigarettes and drinking gallons of tea, as soon as Abhi saw Dhanu and Priya coming towards us he signaled me and I immediately threw away the cigarette in my hand.

Abhi gave them a grin and welcomed.

"You rascals what are you doing over here, why didn't you come to the room?" Dhanu yelled at us.

"We were waiting for you peoples only; I was having some work in college so Mit and I went there" Abhi says while relaxing more in the chair.

"And why was your mobile off Mit?" Priya asked

"Oh, I just forgot to charge it last night" I mumbled.

So, we passed some more time there and moved to the room .

Months just passed so rapidly. Priya helped all of us by making our study schedule and stopping us to get involved in gossip, as leaves passed exam period was also passed with lot of chaos and plenty of dilemmas and as it finished we were ready to enjoy holidays.

As holidays started Priya and Abhi went to their homes, Priya to Pune and Abhi to Satara. Dhanu and I continued our scheduled meetings at college katta.

7
PRIYA'S NEW ROOM

A brand new year started and as expected Abhi landed in the city before college started. Our college katta conferences started we used to sit their till midnight every day, gossiping on versatile topics. Now we had no fear of results may be it was because we were matured enough now or may be because we were stronger.

Results were declared Abhi, Dhanu and I were the happiest persons on the earth as we had passed our first year. Priya topped her class, Dhanu was also amongst the toppers but from the lower side, so I and Abhi did as expected.

College started and Priya expressed her desire to shift in the city she wanted to stay in the city as a paying guest alone so, naturally the responsibility of searching a room for her came upon us.

Primary requirements for the room are as follows.

• Room should be near to Abhi's, my or Dhanu's house.

• Room should have proper air circulation, good water supply and should be having mace facility in it or near to it.

• There should be minimal disturbance from room owner.

So, room search started and after lots of efforts we searched a room it was near to Abhi's room so, first requirement was fulfilled, room is in the row housing owner was living at ground floor and paying guest will be staying in the room on first floor, Abhi and I checked out that room. It was nice room, room owner was a 55 something years old lady living there alone in that house so, she wanted a girl as a paying guest to give her company.

That lady, named Lalitabai, we used to call her aunty was a typical Orthodox woman with white hair and white sari her husband is was dead and son was working in another city and used to visit her every three months so aunty was living alone from some years and that loneliness has made her somewhat harsh and ruthless but it didn't matters as we did not have to deal with her too much. We paid her deposit and on one Sunday we shifted Priya with her luggage to that room.

So, our routine started with attending college in morning and gathering at Abhi's room's terrace or Priya's room in the evening.

Days were going so smoothly, bunking classes for movies, picnic like vital activities were on their way, and as Priya's new room was in the city now our frequent visits to her room increased as being boys we were not having any sense of time and our visit to a girl at any time started making her orthodox room owner Lalitabai upset.

In the beginning, she used to give us somewhat obnoxious look but we ignored it considering it her natural stance for welcoming peoples but one day when we planned for a movie at 9:30 night which was a last show and Priya came back at the midnight and Dhanu dropped her. And obviously, they used to chat for about an half hour at the gate of house. Lalitabai was carefully observing each and every movement of this Love pair without coming in their knowledge from her window.

Priya said Goodbye to Dhanu when it was 12:30 of midnight and moved to get into her room suddenly one voice came from backside which was calling her by taking her name Priya turned back to see who is calling, and it was Lalitabai calling her from window.

"What happened Lalitabai?" Priya asked while going closer to the window.

"Priya, come inside. I want to talk to you about something important, come my door is open" Lalitabai said in a somewhat rude voice.

Priya went inside her room.

"Have a seat Priya" Lalitabai indicated a chair placed in one corner and herself sat on the sofa kept in front of the chair.

"Priya you are like my daughter. If I had a daughter she would be of your age only" Lalitabai said in a soft voice.

"Yes, Lalitabai. I know that you are a good caring mother." Priya tried to satisfy her ego.

"Yes, Priya as a caring mother I have the same feelings for you which I posses for my son, you are living away from your parents they would be thinking of you every minute, you have a responsibility on you that their faith on you should not be wasted"

"Yes, Lalitabai I know that. Please be direct what do you want to say?" Priya's eagerness to know exactly what's going on in Lalitabai's mind was at its peak.

"Priya I don't like your late night hanging out with boys, you also spend all of your day time with those boys and hanging out till late night with them, its not good for a girl living in a new city alone child, what peoples will think about it, it would be better to be getting alert before someone points a finger at your character for that." Lalitabai let out all the storm thundering in her mind from the first day she saw us.

"Lalitabai don't misunderstand them. They are my good friends. I know them very well and I know you are saying this because of your concern only but don't worry I know my responsibility very well". Priya tried to close the matter and ignore what Lalitabai is saying by making this statement and of course this was going to hurt the ego of that old lady.

"Look Priya I fulfilled my responsibilities by saying this to you. After all, I owe you nothing but I was feeling some social responsibilities towards this matter that's why I told you all this after this it's your decision what to do, but keep it in mind boys will be always boys and a girl has nothing with her if she does not have a good character" says Lalitabai.

"Lalitabai, my parents are there to think about me. You don't need to make these efforts, and I am from a good, respected family. You mind your own business" Priya rapidly went to her room in anger after saying this she forcefully pulled the door, which made a thunderous noise after collapsing with wall.

Priya went to her room and cried for a while. It was first time in her life that someone had embarrassed her by pointing towards her behavior or her way of living her life. Priya was a very cool, modern, and free minded girl she had grown up in a modern atmosphere in Pune where her parents were Doctors and always gave her freedom to choose her friends, to live her life the way she wanted. They never had interfered in their daughter's personal life as they knew her very well from her childhood.

By nature Priya was a modest girl but she would never tolerate that someone was blaming her friends. That was the reason she rudely answered Lalitabai and got out of that place angrily.

Next day Priya called me Abhi and Dhanu and asked them to gather at Abhi's room

I got a little late and Priya, Abhi and Dhanu were already waiting for me as I came Priya explained all incidents of late night twist with moist eyes.

"hey, Priya that old lady has gone mad. Don't think too much about her, she doesn't deserve that" Said Abhi registering first official reaction to Priya.

"Abhi is right Priya. Just ignore her." Said Dhanu.

"How could I, you all know no one has talked to me like this ever then why should I tolerate her for the sake of that room only?" Priya seemed to be very aggrieved now.

"Look Priya, practically speaking right now we have no option because at this period of time there is no such room available in this area for a single girl so, until we find something else, the only option you have is to stick with it and as for the matter of your tiff with her, you can talk about it to your mom and dad. They will definitely help you to come out of that" I said giving her my condolences.

"I think you are right Mit I will try" said Priya.

"Hey Mit you are a gem yaar I knew it you will do something" Abhi with joy.

"And Priya don't talk much with her and don't get involved in any foolish arguments" now its Dr. Dhanu.

"Okay, I understand don't worry much about this I will try to adjust and I am absolutely fine now" said Priya

"Okay, then lets go and celebrate yaar lets go to US pizza today" Abhi with same excitement

"Hey, is it your birthday Dracula?" I yelled at him.

"No yaar, I am in a mood for celebration" justified Abhi.

So after some discussion proposal was accepted by the decision making committee of Priya and our army moved to the pizza house.

After some days I got the news of ceasefire between Lalitabai and Priya. I could guess it easily that war is not still over.

8

ANNUAL FUNCTION AND A PROMISE

It was a last year of my and Abhi's academic course, Priya and Dhanu still had one more year to go. Days came and went very fast just like the girls in the Abhi's life.

One afternoon Dhanu, me, Priya and Abhi, were gathered after bunking class to plan evening's party and don't ask why because it was in the honor of Abhi's 6th girlfriend.

"I don't think this asshole will be loyal to someone in his life." I said sitting on the chair in kaki's canteen and pointing to Abhi.

"Fuck with your loyalty yaar. I am not running a charity trust to show loyalty and girls always leave me first. I didn't ever ditch a girl in my life" Abhi reacted abruptly.

"Will you let me know why?" I asked.

"Well,.. I don't like their prosthetic faces and always behaving like a delicate doll, and you know these girls always has a self-interest while making friendship or developing relationship with a guy and that self-interest may be regarding money, or just a desire to have a boyfriend or a desire to have a company of boy who will entertain you and do whatever you like or it may be for the sake of physical relation only" Abhi was again in the loveguru mode.

"It's sick yaar" says Priya

"And Dhanu you are the luckiest guy I ever saw on this planet earth. You have a girl who is beyond all this, she is perfect! And don't ever leave her alone friend otherwise I will kill you" Abhi's eyes were looking dreamy while saying this.

"I know Abhi I have a real gem. I will never let her go from my life" Dhanu responded.

"Hey guys! have you seen any romantic English drama or decided to play a prank on me" Priya joked.

"Its real Priya you don't know what you are, this Abhi baba says you will be an excellent mother, a great housewife in future and if I was there in place of Dhanu I would be the luckiest man of the earth and by god I would never have this flirty attitude. I would be a simple guy like Dhanu" says Abhi.

"Okay, Baba Abhi Baba accepted, now tell us what to do for your so called prosthetic faced girlfriend" Priya says while closing her palms in prayer in front of Abhi.

"What to do yaar, I will tell her that our plan is cancelled and we will go to the movie in the night show" says Abhi.

"Abhi, you are unpredictable, Asshole" I said while giving him a glare.

After movie Priya was dropped to her room by Dhanu and we used to seat and chat on college katta as per our regular routine, I and Abhi were having a cigarette and dhanu came.

"hey, give me a puff" Dhanu yelled from bike itself.

"have it" I offered y cigarette to him.

"Hey, Abhi I wanna ask you something" Dhanu said

"ask baby"

"hey, how many times did you had a sex" Dhanu asked

"umm… I have to count it yaar…. I think it might be thrice"

"how it feels after that"

"umm.. nothing yaar but it's a feeling of completeness, one feels like oh!, its my body and all parts of it are working, that's it but why did you asking these fucking questions rascal, is there anything going in your mind?"

"no.. nothing yaar I just wanna know how it feels"

"look Dhanu just having sex is nothing bigger but having it with a girl you loves most is a great pleasure in the world but keep it in mind my friend don't ever abuse someone's trust on you because feeling of trust is much more important ever, than a physical relation, just look at me yaar I have had a physical relation with so many girls but still having no one's true love and no one's trust in me so I am on bloody looser side" Abhi is speaking like a mature boy.

"Hey, you rascal we are having trust on you, you are our gem, but just sometimes behaves like a asshole" I replied to wind up the discussion and it is ended with lots of smiles.

It was a February month a time prior to start of PL and final exams and by all the ways time of annual functions, like every year Abhi me and Dhanu as being the members of BBA which is "back benchers association" were playing a role of responsible and supporting audiences by seating on the backbench and encouraging them by our mind blowing claps and mock s.

It was Dhanu and Priya's college Gathering and this year Priya decided to dance on a song and the convincing force behind this was of course ours.

We enthusiastically helped her in her preparations by dropping her for rehearsals on time (?) by going to pick up her from their and by becoming first audience of her dance she was excellent dancer but not passionate about that she was dancing this time because it was a last year of mine and Abhi and it's a gift to us from her.

As usual we entered late at the gathering hall where all the programs were going on we desperately went to the stage side by cutting all the rush over there we were not knowing whats exactly going on and when was Priya's dance so we asked a weird faced boy wondering on the stage.

"When was the Priya's dance?"

"Which Priya?"

"Priya from First years MCS"

"Oh, that will require lots of time there is prize distribution ceremony before that" he told us the schedule.

"we are cursed man, this prize distribution will suck us I never had attended a full length annual function" said Abhi exasperatingly.

"So do I yaar there is no point in standing in this crowd of fools like assholes" I also expressed my Depression.

"Okay, then lets get out and will try to come before Priya's dance" Dhanu suggested.

We moved towards a canteen and used to seat their

"Hey Dhanu order a ciggy" Abhi said, ciggy is a pet name given by us to a cigarette.

"hi, friends having fun in the canteen?" a voice came from the backside so we looked back he was Ravi he is Dhanu and Priya's classmate and a real bastard, he was like a villain of old hindi movies always having a mob of three to four weird faced boys with him and as his father is politician he had some attitude and bad habit of underestimating everyone, Ravi was always jealous on Dhanu as he had ravish girl of his class with him and this is the right time he found for mocking as Priya is not there.

"Hi, Ravi the leader, hey Mit take a chair see future MLA comes to meet us" Abhi Scoffed at him.

"Oh! Abhi you are only three where is your cheerleader I couldn't see her anywhere" He used the chance of scoffing on Priya, and now he has crossed the limits.

"Hey, Ravi mind your fucking tongue bastard" Abhi spluttered with anger.

"hey.. hey guys please calm down there is no reason to fight yaar, we all has very few days to spent here and we using them to indulge it in nonsense things" Dhanu tried to hinder the situation.

"Dhanu tell your friends don't mess with me, stay in your limits" Ravi mumbled and stood up to go.

"Ravi, clap doesn't sounds with one hand you also take care of your words" I pointed his mistake.

Ravi gone by his way but matter is not resolved still Abhi is burning in fire in his inner side and the victim of his anger is going to be now poor chap Dhanu as Ravi is not there.

Abhi gone and sat on his bike I and Dhanu ran behind him "Hey, Abhi what happen? Where are you going dude?" Dhanu asked.

Abhi kicked bike and said "Let's go".

"but where dude" I asked as I was worried whether he is going behind that rascal Ravi to mess with him.

"Let's go yaar don't ask anything further" Abhi spluttered giving a rough glare at Dhanu his face become ruddy we quickly sat on the bike and Abhi accelerated.

"Where are we going Abhi?" I asked as he was racing the bike like never before.

"To anna's Dhaba" Abhi spoke finally but something unexpected.

"Oh god this chap gone mad, bloody fool did you forget there is priya's Dance after an hour and you are going to drink that bloody bear" now I was on fire I knew that at this moment my words will not affect him much but it was necessary to realize him about the situation.

Abhi was in no situation to talk he was just concentrated on his driving, I looked behind to Dhanu he was trying to look at tires of the bike and seems to be in the mood of let happened what's happening around.

We came to the Anna's Dhaba it was seven thirty of evening Abhi walked to our fix table quickly Dhanu and I followed him, we sat on the chairs. "Golu, One Kingfisher strong and fast" Abhi ordered in little bit rough voice, I have first time seen him in such mood he was trying to look in the water in the glass kept in front of him I tried to search whether he has discovered anything there by tilting my head little bit but I found nothing except his one more rough glare.

"stop this nonsense Mit" Abhi spluttered.

"I think this sentence must be mine" I answered smartly.

"Chilled bear Abhi bhai" Golu kept bottle of Bear in front of

Abhi and opened it with a opener hanged in his neck.

"Are you going to drink alone bloody fool? Golu bring one more" it was a comeback of Dhanu.

"Oh good, no its great now we are going to drink here like fucking losers and Priya will curse us tomorrow for not being there at the time of her dance" I cursed them both.

"Then what will I do yaar! Tell this silly chap" Dhanu flashed.

"Oh, then you are blaming me and why didn't you speak like this in front of Ravi?"

"I felt no necessity of that; I don't give him so much importance that I should mind his any statement. Look Dhanu, Ravi is jealous of us because despite having everything he is incomplete, he is incomplete because he does not have friends like us with him. He has a group of guys with him at all times but he trusts nobody. That's why he feels like a loser when he sees us, and there is no need of giving importance to such a sick guy" Dhanu completed and I was totally shocked.

"Oh god it's you Dhanu!" I was surprised Dhanu was being so mature. I could definitely see the effect of Priya in his tone, it was Priya who was speaking through his mouth.

Dhanu smiled in response to me, beer came and was served in two glasses.

"Mit you will not drink?" Abhi asked

"No yaar I am not in the mood"

"Oh then it's because of me only" Abhi said.

"No yaar, really I don't want to".

"Drink you devil otherwise I will also not take it"

"Me niether" Dhanu joined him.

"Hey bring one more glass fast" Abhi ordered and I joined the party of fools.

After four beers we realized about Priya's dance "oh, shit man its eight forty five" Dhanu shouted.

"Hey wait for a while yaar I want to try some rum" Abhi suggested

"It will be cocktail bloody fool! You already had a beer" I tried to convince him but it was useless. Abhi ordered rum "Try it yaar, its also good" he poured rum in our empty glasses of beer "thirty, thirty, thirty total ninety ml okay take this little dose and we will immediately go to the college" remaining space in glass was filled by thums up and Abhi prepared a drink for us. It was our first time having rum. I was really nervous inside but some moments are unstoppable and you just flow with the momentum.

After finishing our drinks we moved to our bike. We were completely wasted.

"Hey Mit, I am hungry yaar" Dhanu revealed his situation.

"We have no choice yaar, we have to leave. We will have food later. Let's move fast" I started bike and both fools sat on the seat.

"Hey drive slow Mit. You are drunk you know na?" now it was

Abhi revealing his situation.

Finally we managed to reach at hall program was on its way. Pupils were enjoying we moved fast from crowd and went near the stage actually we needed very less effort to move from the crowd thanks to our Rum + beer cocktail which made pupils to give us way. Smell of rum started to indicate presence of three drunk fools in the crowd and it became more effective because of compact atmosphere of hall I also heard some girly sounds of 'oh' 'uuh' 'shit' from the crowd but we were not in the mood of wasting time in silly things so we just moved.

And announcement was made "Next performer is Priya joshi from first year MCS" claps become louder and there was priya, oh god she was looking marvelous she has wore decent white salwar with silver starry bindis on it she was looking charming just like a angel.

Song started it was Falguni pathak's song "Oh piya, oh piya leke doliya..." Falguni's voice was sweet and so was Priya dance too.

"Hey, let's go there back. We can stand on benches there" Abhi pointed towards backside benches and of course we moved there, we stood on the benches. It was very hard for us to stand there in this situation but Priya's dance made us to forget that pain as Priya and her dance both were rocking "Hey dude Priya is a good dancer ha" someone gave his compliment to Dhanu and Dhanu moved his head with a smile like a father smiles when his child dances for the first time on stage.

"Hey dude look the cheer girl is dancing on the stage yaar" voice came from one corner Ravi was standing there with his friends.

"Hey Dhanu go man she is calling you there! Oh piya, oh piya, oh piya" Ravi laughed vigorously scoffing again towards us, from his group joined in laughing someone yelled at us "Oh piya, oh piya".

"You bastard" Abhi shouted in anger and attacked Ravi suddenly, he kicked his stomach strongly with left knee. Ravi collapsed on the ground holding stomach with both hands, Ravi's friends attacked Abhi but I and dhanu pushed them back, the guys some time ago giving lessons on morals were now fighting with same aggression as of Abhi's what a mess I don't know whether it's a impact of cocktail or it's a pure friendship which worked, I was having no feeling in my mind to hit anybody but my only intention was to save my friend from being hit by Ravi's friends. Attention of crowd drawn towards us as noise went to the level of song, some healthy pupils from crowd aggressively interfered in between and separated Abhi and Ravi from each other we were also pushed back by the crowd "hey who is there? What's going on there?" a rough and matured voice came from front side and it was Prof. Gaikwad Principal of Abhi's college he came towards us Abhi was still held by some healthy students by grabbing his both hands towards his back and Ravi was sitting to side by still holding his stomach with facial expressions showing pain, this bastard is doing another drama I thought in mind but we cant do anything on that as its he who's stomach got hit and he only can judge about the pain.

Prof. was looking angry he came towards us "What the hell is going on over here? Is this a reason you guys wanted annual function to dig out your personal revenges, who are that bastards?" the boy holding Abhi presented him in front of Prof. Gaikwad just like war prisoner is presented in front of king at the end of war and its up to king to make a decision whether he wanted to kill that prisoner or give him a mercy and really now its upon Prof.

Prof. came in front of Abhi just like Alexander came in front of Porus to ask him what type of treatment he should give him as a prisoner of war and the thing which I am worried was ensued, our almighty Alexander found our so called great king Porus drunk, Abhi's gesture was enough for anybody to tell that he was drunk but the smell of Rum was doing his work from distance.

"Mr. Abhishek Patil you are drunk, you came in my college drunk and beating students here in annual function in front of our guests, you know people like you should never be allowed to get admitted in Professional courses like Engineering but you peoples manages everything with the money but I tell you I will never let you pass this year so easily and this is my promise to you Mr. Patil" Prof. Gaikwad finished by pointing finger towards Abhi's face, and for sure he was looking definitely in serious mood and this person is really of that kind if he likes someone he will build his life and if he messes with someone he could destroy his life with no mercy.

"Sir, first tell that Bastard he started all this" Abhi spluttered in arrogant voice.

"Shut up, you don't need to tell me what should I do" Prof. Gaikwad warned again then he moved towards Ravi. "Mr. Ravi this is not your dads political stage, this is last warning for you next time any silly mistake from both of you will lead to the suspension from college, mind it" Prof. finished his session and went towards stage the boy holding Abhi released him.

"I will see you buffalo" Abhi spluttered on boy holding him he was still in aggressive mode which indicated that Cocktail was still doing his job.

Gathering was finished for us and we are out of the gate now sitting on college stairs with one ciggy shared in three of us there is silence maintained among us as no one is in the mood of explaining anything again everything went wrong over there.

"Hey don't tell it to priya ha" Abhi said while releasing circle of smoke in the air.

"She may have got known everything bloody fool, her dance was interrupted for a while because of this" Dhanu realized him situation while taking charge of cigarette from him.

"Shut up guys just don't justify anything to her try to let it go off" I interrupted their conversation.

Dhanu's mobile rang "hey, its priya keep quite" Dhanu picked up the phone "Hey, priya ......we are here on canteen stairs ....okay we are coming there ...just in a minute okay, fine" I was observing Dhanu while he is speaking with priya he is behaving like a nursery boy talks with his mom when he had done any mistake and afraid that his mom is knowing about that. It was a same expression when Dhanu talks with his mom on phone when he was drunk and gives excuses for not coming to home for dinner, Dhanu's mother is strict may be because she is a Lawyer and she think that she knows world better than anyone else.

"Hey, guys lets go Priya is waiting at college gate" Dhanu sat on bike Abhi stood up throwing a cigarette.

"hey wash your hands fool" I yelled at them washing hands and taking one mint candy after having a ciggy is our routine procedure and we cannot deviate from that it was a unwritten law.

We reached at college gate annual gathering was finished no one is there in campus Priya was waiting for us at the gate holding a bag with both hands, she looked at us as our bikes reached near her I found her face emotionless and that means she is angry.

Dhanu stopped his bike near her and she quietly sat on the bike Dhanu is having no guts to say anything so I said "hey, Priya your dance was really good yaar and your song selection is also nice" I was trying hard to be innocent.

"Oh, that means you guys got the time to watch the dance also" Oh shit man she is really angry I used to keep quite then, we moved to our katta spot and our bikes stopped.

"guys I want to speak with you get down" said Priya while seating at katta.

"Did you want to discuss about that bloody fight with the bastards" Abhi said while seating on the bike and one leg on kick.

"No, not at all how can I dare for that Mr. Patil" said Priya her sentence is indication that she is still angry.

"Hey, priya don't call me that Mr. Patil, it remembers me Prof. Gaikwad" Abhi complained in childish voice.

"Okay, forget that all I don't want to listen anything about your silly bullfight but I want just one promise from you all" Priya pointing her finger and I recalled prof. Gaikwad warning Abhi by pointing finger at him.

"What?" we asked in chorus.

"Give me promise that you three of you won't drink that alcohol again" Priya's voice was firm.

"Oh, that's enough Priya you are behaving like Dhanu's mom now" Abhi replied in irritated voice.

"No, I am not its necessary to have control on you guys, promise me otherwise I will not speak with you all" Priya

"Including me?" Dhanu questioned like surprised. "Yes including you, you are not anyone different"

"Priya, but we will not let such things happen next time please yaar…." Abhi still finding way to escape from making promise.

"No I am not sure about you guys you will never change"

"Hey, Mit speak something na yaar why are you standing and

watching all this quietly" Abhi now approached me for seeking help, because he knows Priya will at least listen me carefully but I am afraid as I am also a culprit at this time.

"umm.. Priya okay, you are right but give some excuse yaar" I am not sure that she will listen anything that's why my voice was not firm.

"Okay, in future if you plans any party I must be included in it"

"Hey whats this Priya how could we drink in front of you?" Abhi spluttered.

"Okay, then don't drink its clear if you wanna drink, I will be with you if you have problem in that then don't drink" Priya was firm on her decision and this is not a good time for argue so I agreed immediately.

"Okay, Priya agree as you say" I raised the thumb.

"Hey, Mit whats this man" Abhi spluttered again.

"Shut up Abhi close the discussion and lets go" I pointed him to start the bike.

That discussion was closed but it took some days to convince priya.

9
RESULTS, JOB AND THE LAST PARTY

Final year gone with lots of joy, celebration and at same time tensions and usual nightmares during exam periods. Time passed away but left the memories behind, memories which are having blossom of true friendship, memories of celebrations we did with each other and some unforgotten moments of shared joy. We through our exams with our all time tested and approved One night show pattern, it was my and Abhi's last year but Dhanu and Priya still have one year of their MCS so we were waiting for my and Abhi's results eagerly.

It was Abhi's result first, I was with him we went to his college Abhi stopped his bike near canteen. "Hey Abhi lets go dude" I said surprisingly.

"Wait yaar results won't go anywhere let's have a cigarette first" Abhi, while parking bike.

We used to seat on the canteen chairs and ordered our all time favorite combination tea with a ciggy.

"Hey, Mit have you planned anything?" Said Abhi while taking a first puff.

"Anything what ?"

"I mean to say after getting this fucking degree what you have planned, going to do a job or any other fucking option of get sucked for two more years in doing masters"

"No, way yaar I had left that option of doing M. Pharma or MBA so far behind, otherwise I will be preparing for GATE instead of hanging out with you"

"Then job ?"

"yeah, I have to think over that seriously, after all I have to use that degree somewhere and my parents are having some expectations, that their son will earn some four figure salary soon after passing B. Pharma"

"Yeah, so you should try for job Eh,"

"And what you planned?"

"Just nothing yaar my mind is still blank, I am worried about my results first" Abhi made a ring of smoke and released in air, it's a sign that he is tense.

"Leave it bloody fucker stop making rings of smoke and go to collect the results" I spluttered

"Okay you stop here I will be just back" Abhi stood up to go mashed cigarette with foot.

I waited there for next 10 minutes and my phone rang it was Abhi "Hey Mit, Prof. Gaikwad kept his promise".

"Promise? What Promise?" I asked inquisitively.

"he kept my practical's yaar" Abhi answered

"How many subjects?"

"Two"

"Okay, fuck it off come here soon" I tried to give negligence to result matter just to keep moment wispy.

Abhi came with mark sheet rolled and held in one hand and his usual trade mark smile on face. "Hey, it will took one more year for me to become an engineer"

"Yeah, and meanwhile you can think over what's next" Abhi nodded and we burst into laugh.

Now after just one week of Abhi's results it's a time of my judgment day and this time Priya Dhanu and Abhi decided to company me to get the results, I was remembering my first day in the school when my mother and some two to three lady neighbors came to drop me in the school. "Hey, guys are you kidding with me?" I sound irritatingly.

"No, yaar we are just accompanying you" said Dhanu

"yaar, I am feeling like a four year child going to school first time, stop this nonsense and seat in canteen I will come to you" I spluttered.

"Okay, lets go lets have a ....Tea first then go" Abhi trying to speak about cigarette but his mind suddenly got aware of the presence of Priya and word ciggy turned to Tea.

"Okay, guys lets go" said Priya.

"I got a call from a Pharma MNC yesterday" I revealed a secret.

"Oh, it's great Mit, Job offer before results, then what happened" Priya keyed up.

"Nothing great they took my telephonic interview, they short listed my resume from resumes sent by college" I replied.

"What did he asked in the interview?" Priya

"Yeah, some general questions on background some part from academic, I through the interview but I can join them only after sending my final year mark sheet by courier after that only they will send Offer letter" I unfold the whole story of my placement.

"You bloody devil it means that if you passes Final year you will got automatically placed, you had a job with you before passing final year and you are telling in this way!" Abhi thrown a small stone towards me to register his anger but it was he because of whom I didn't shared this with that excitement with which it should be shared, Abhi's failure disappointed me moreover the thing which disappointed me is that he has to stay back there for giving his back subjects which he has passed only because of his practical's are not cleared this is total injustice to him, but this thing didn't affected Abhi at all, he is enjoying as usual, this is Abhi I know he will definitely utilize this time.

"Hey devil are you scared of results?" Abhi shouted at me.

"No way yaar just thinking" I replied while standing up "lets go I will come with you" says Abhi.

We proceeded towards college building "Hey come soon guys we are waiting here" Priya gave a call from back.

Abhi and I went to the Office registrar to collect mark sheet "Mr. Maitreya you are passed" Registrar revealed the most awaited secret easily in his usual tone. Abhi took that mark sheet from him excitedly.

"Yes! Mit party tonight" Abhi yelled and I just chuckled.

It was really a party time, after suffering for four years in the same old and frustrating education system I am entering into the world of reality where no one will judge me with the stupid, useless and unpractical questions which are having no relation with the real practical world, now I will learn the real things, now the world around me will be my school, I was happy but same time I was in hurry, I have to join in Ahmedabad day after tomorrow so, I have to pack just in one day and one night is there for partying so we started my packing quickly Priya came to my house to help me, after being satisfied that everything is okay she left my home at evening for getting ready for nights party.

Party place was fixed as Abhi's room, it is absolutely Priya's Idea to celebrate at room itself, we got disappointed but after all its high commands decision so, we have to follow it.

I reached at room late it was 8:30 pm Abhi, Priya and Dhanu were already waiting for me "Hey devil you are 30 minutes late" Abhi showed his clock "I know you have Rolex don't show it" I scoffed at him.

"I am showing you time fool" Abhi replied.

"Hey, what's today's menu friends?" I questioned eagerly as my stomach is crying for food.

"Every thing is there, her highness madam priya selected every thing starting from soup which madam Priya cooked herself, after that there is fresh mutter paneer, Punjabi dum aloo, Dal tadka, jeera rice, and fresh rotis all ordered packed and brought by Madam Priya" Dhanu counted every item kept on dining table in a posture of waiter of any five star hotel I concluded he will never remain jobless he has good qualities of being waiter.

"Thank you so much Mr. Dhanu" Priya said delightedly.

"Hey, Priya wait yaar before starting this I want to remind you something" Abhi interfered when Priya was moving ahead to open Tiffin of soup.

"What?" Priya questioned.

"Priya did you remember that you took one promise from us?" Abhi trying to recall her something with childish face.

"What promise?" Priya was still in bewilderment and even we do.

"That promise which you took from us on that annual function night that we will not drink and if we will drink you must be present there" now the mystery is opened and Abhis face was like he has opened a big secret which will become beneficial to the mankind, here not to the mankind but definitely it will become beneficial to the three of us.

"Oh! That's the thing you want to speak, and for that only you are suggesting to party outside" says Priya

"Yeah priya, but believe me only because Mit is leaving its just for enjoying yaar please allow we will not drink much" Abhi had now joined both hands one joins for praying god and bent on his knees, this is Abhi a true actor.

"Okay, but if Mit agrees and if you drinks very small" priya agreed but thrown ball in my court now.

"Yeah!" Abhi and dhanu yelled in joy and Abhi came to me and held my shoulders "Hey Mit devil don't let e ask you that you are agreed or not"

"Yeah, its okay yaar, Priya let us do that for today only" I was already ion the band of baddies so there is no way to escape.

Abhi immediately drawn a bottle of Vodka kept in his suitcase and another one liter fridgepack of sprite from his fridge.

"That means you had planned everything bastard" I was stunned to look at his preparation and even Priya was.

"yes my dear, I am always ready I knew it today is the only day when Priya couldn't stop us from enjoying so why not to take the benefit of the situation after all someone had said it well do the jiggy when your time comes so I am doing" Abhi shaked his ass in joy while holding bottle of vodka in one hand and Priya and I were burst into the laugh.

"Hey, its apple favor dude smell it" Abhi smelled the aroma by opening lid of bottle and handed over it to Dhanu.

Drink was served by Abhi he made the glasses for three and poured cold drink in fourth glass for Priya.

"Okay, lets Cheers friends for the bright career of Mit" Abhi announced and raised the glass for cheers, all four hands were raised and party began.

Priya stopped the drinking session when everyone finished two glasses each.

"okay, its enough guys you enjoyed a lot noe pack up your drinking session and move to eat" Priya is now in charge.

"Its not enough Priya just one peg more" Dhanu is now in answerable mode that means vodka is doing its job.

"No way, stop drinking otherwise I will leave from here" Priya now threatened us this is her last weapon for sure.

"Okay, Okay guys we have enjoyed a lot now let's move to eat" Abhi surrendered raising his both hands in air, and Dhanu also kept his glass.

"Okay, then move to eat I am so hungry Priya" Dhanu moved towards Priya and sat beside her.

Priya served four plates and dinner started it was nice balanced party unlike our all previous parties it was 11:30 when we finished eating and Priya said

"Lets go guys I am leaving who is coming to drop me?" Priya asked this question while staring at dhanu just to check his reactions.

"Obviously Dhanu yaar, Dhanu go and come fast we will have a walk towards college road" Abhi looked at dhanu while getting relaxed in the chair.

"Okay, lets go Priya" Dhanu jumped and collected the keys.

They reached at Priya's room Lalita bai's rooms door was closed but her light was on, Dhanu stopped bike in front of the gate Priya moved away from Dhanu to go, and Dhanu hold her hand "Hey, Priya don't go like this, say something before leaving" Dhanu demanded in childish way.

"Something, something what?" Priya questioned as she is naïve but she knows what's going around in Dhanu's mind.

"Something for instance you can say umm…I will miss you"

"Okay any thing else?"

"yeah you can say goodnight, sweet dreams"

"Nice, any thing more"

"Or you can say I love you"

"Eh, I will not say that"

"But why?"

"Its my mouth I will say only what I will like to say" Priya is now willfully hanging Dhanu

"Ah, why you are always doing that, please say ones" Dhanu's face become lamentable.

Priya chuckled and removed her hand from Dhanu's grip and proceeded towards steps to get into her room Dhanu desperately pursued her, Priya entered in her room and Dhanu followed her.

"Dhanu please go, I am tired now and I wanted to go to bed now" said Priya in a manner to avoid Dhanu but a naughty smile was still on her face.

Dhanu came forward and held her hand again now Priya is immovable she doesn't reacted at all, her body become warm, Dhanu now pulled her towards him and hold her waist with his left hand, Priya was still looking at ground Dhanu pulled her more closer, now they can clearly listen each other's breath sounds, some seconds gone in this posture and suddenly Priya broken down into Dhanu's clasp.

"Hey, my angel can I do it now?" Dhanu murmured into Priya's ears.

"What?" Priya asked holding him some more tightly.

"You know" Dhanu says.

"Then why are you asking for, I am your now and forever for, ever and ever" Priya mumbling with closed eyes.

Now Dhanu held her hairs with right hand and brought her face closure to his, Priya's eyes were closed he kept his lips on her lips and they started smooching like never before.

Dhanu grabbed her and placed her body on bed now Priya is participating actively with Dhanu, time lapsed he was in and they did it, Dhanu and Priya crossed all their borders, the borders of physical relations now their relationship reached on its destination it become complete, they are two bodies with the one soul now.

Here two hours passed we were waiting for Dhanu, now Abhi started to become hyper "Hey, why that asshole taking so time to come?" Abhi murmured.

"He might be busy in chatting with Priya" I explained.

"But look at the time yaar two hours were passed already, this is not the way to behave yaar" Abhi is still upset, I seen him first time thinking on any issue in such a way.

"Why are you being so hyper Abhi?, He will come yaar I am going to sleep come whenever you feels like sleepy okay, goodnight" I called for the day and proceed towards bed.

Abhi waited there by seating on the chair but he didn't called Dhanu on his cell, I don't what was going around in his mind but definitely he had sensed something.

Here Dhanu and Priya had forgot the world around them Dhanu is slept in the bed watching at the fan revolving on his head, and Priya half lying on his body by placing her head on Dhanu's chest her hands were moving through the jungle area of Dhanu's chest both were enjoying the magic of that moment they were feeling the joy of being together.

"Priya, I just remembered Dhanu's one sentence he used to say me one day" Dhanu said while moving his hand in Priya's hairs.

"What sentence?" Priya muttered.

"He said me once 'Dhanu, having sex is not a great thing but having it with the one whom you loves most is the greatest pleasure in the world' and Priya at this moment I am feeling that joy I am feeling I am at the top of the world Priya, Oh! So lucky I am and it's only because of you Priya, just because of you" Dhanu said this and kissed Priya's forehead.

"I love you Dhanu" Priya replied in back.

"Eh, I was dying to listen that" Dhanu whispered with surprise.

Priya chuckled and place again her head on Dhanu's chest.

Dhanu looked at the wall clock of his side wall and yelled "Oh, shit Priya its 6:00 of morning"

Priya looked at the clock "I also didn't felt how time passed; you must go Dhanu Lalitabai might be aroused"

Dhanu wore his cloths and proceed towards the door to open it while Priya is still laid on the bed Dhanu turned back "Hey, angel goodbye"

"Goodbye Dhanu" Priya threw a flying kiss.

Dhanu started to go down through stairs Lalitabai's door was opened Dhanu immediately went towards the gate to open it quietly but the gate did noise which was sufficient to signal Lalitabai, Dhanu closed the gate and sat on his bike and suddenly Lalitabai came out of her room to see who opened her gate, Dhanu immediately started his bike and took a turn Lalita bai came near the gate to see him but he rapidly vanished on the bike Lalitabai understood that this boy came from the girls room who is living as paying guest in her room.

"What the time came there is no control at all on today's children's parents send them to study out of the home and what are they doing here, Oh, god if I had such a child I will definitely have killed her Oh, god save" Lalitabai mumbled to herself she is not having any other way to protest as she is not having any clue that the boy came from girls room only she has not seen him while coming, so she used to go to her work while mumbling to herself.

Here my eyes opened due to Dhanu's bikes sound I opened the door and Dhanu is standing in front of me with smile on face he was looking damn fresh "Good morning Mit"

"what so good about the morning?' I replied

"Hey, by the way where were you whole night Abhi was waiting for you yaar, at least you should inform to us that you are going to home for sleeping" I just recalled about the night and spluttered on him.

"Sorry yaar but I was not at my home" Dhanu replied.

"Then, where were you for the whole night?" I became more curious.

"I was at Priya's room I was with her for the whole night" Dhanu answered with same smile on the face.

I was stunned my mouth remained opened for a while "Then you did that?" I asked.

"Umm... actually Yeah we did that" Dhanu said while looking at the ground.

Dhanu sat on the chair quite relaxed and then he told the whole story of last night.

"Did you use protection Dhanu?" I asked at the end.

"What the hell protection is?, I mean we love each other we will marry with each other and the most important is we trust each other then who cares about that fucking protection yaar" Dhanu spluttered very casually.

"You did wrong Dhanu, you should not have did that" Abhi's voice came from the back; he yelled from the bed he was listening our whole conversation.

Dhanu turned towards Abhi "Hey, what fucking wrong I did, why the hell you both are blaming on me I mean what different thing I did, I did the thing which every lover does then what's wrong in this yaar" Dhanu's face now turned like a innocent person who was held for a crime which he hasn't did.

"Don't falsely justify Dhanu, you hadn't did wrong but you did at the wrong time in wrong way, at least you should be bothered about the protection" I spluttered.

"I was worried about this only, Dhanu Priya is innocent girl and she just wanted to prove her love for you at least you should care for her yaar" Abhi tried to show Dhanu's mistake again.

"What the fucking things you are telling to me guys, I care for her and I will tackle everything, you need not to care about that" Dhanu yelled at Abhi now the discussion is turning into a debate.

"What the fuck you are talking Dhanu.." Abhi started to argue on Dhanu's comment but I interfered in between.

"Hey, guys leave this matter here only, Abhi now this is Dhanu and Priya's personal matter you cant say him like this leave the subject here only" I turned my way of speaking Abhi stared at me in shock but it was a right decision to stop the debate despite of letting it to burst into a big battle because I felt that the discussion is hurting Dhanu's ego and which would affect our friendship too so it was good to stop talking on the matter after all Dhanu was right he is capable of handling the situation then we are merely underestimating him.

"And lets go, my train is at 8:00 pm I have to get ready, my parents must be waiting for me, okay bye friends" I went towards the door to leave.

"Hey, wait Mit I will drop you" Dhanu followed me to drop me at my home and Abhi remained their only I thought he must take some time to think over it, after all friendship should also have some limits and close friend should also cant cross these limits.

That night Abhi, Priya and Dhanu came to drop me at the station, Train left the station some hands were moving to say me good bye which are of my dearest friends and my family but my heart is saying goodbye to my city, my Mumbai I will soon be back to you.

10
LIFE AND TWISTS

Meanwhile Surat station passed and I got some space to sit, I looked at luggage point to notice my bag it was still there, a wadapav vendor was selling wadapav's in train. The Train was passing from Surat so here you can find mumbai's famous wada pav's easily as Surat is near to Mumbai and as being Mumbaikar I was missing Mumbai's wadapav from long time in Ahmedabad. So, without wasting a time I called him and brought one from him.

"you can seat here beta" a voice came from back side and I turned back a septuagenarian person seating on window seat was calling me to seat near him, as he was watching me standing at door from long time. I moved to seat there "Halo chacha" I greeted him.

"Hallo beta, tame Gujrati cho?" He asked me in Gujrati.

"Nathi, par Gujrati aavade che" I answered relying on my weak

Gujrati vocabulary.

"Saras" he nodded happily.

"Ghazal bhave che beta?" He asked me whether I like ghazals as he was listening ghazals on his cellphone with help of earphone and he wished to share his one earphone with me.

"Oh, sure chacha which ghazal is that?" I asked while taking earphone from him.

"Sambhal, Sambhal" he asked me to listen it and I took one earphone from him and fitted in my ear oh! This is Ghalibs ghazal and singer is Jagjit great the ghazal was perfect for the journey :

Apni marzi se kaha apne safar ke ham hai, rukh hawao ka jidhar ka udhar ke ha hai

Pahele har cheez thi apni magar ab lagata hai, apne hi ghar me kisi dusre ghar ke ham hai.

It was meaning "I am not a traveler of my own will, I am just flowing with the air,

Initially everything was mine, but now in my own house I am feeling like being in someone else's house". That ghazal dragged me again in my memories.

Here after my leaving to Ahmadabad, Abhi and Dhanu's contacts became very less definitely they were calling me daily but at that time they were not with each other's they were calling me separately.

I got to know from Priya that they are meeting at Our spot 'College katta' it's not like our past days the meetings became like just official meets, most of were because of just Priya's force.

One morning when Dhanu was sleeping in his usual way till 8:00 at morning his cell phone rang. It was Priya calling, he picked up the phone "Hey, honey what's happening? Calling so early?" Dhanu asked in a sleepy voice.

"Dhanu I am afraid, I missed my periods" Priya said in depressed voice from other side.

"Eh, just that and you are waking up me for that?" Dhanu couldn't get rid of the sleep.

"Dhanu, it's not what you are thinking" Priya spluttered.

"Then what?"

"Dhanu, I think I am pregnant" Priya said calmly.

"What?" now Dhanu's sleep ran away in seconds.

"What are you talking about Priya?" are you kidding with me?" Dhanu was still not getting the situation.

"Dhanu I can't joke in this situation I am damn serious please come here soon" Priya said.

"Okay, I am coming. Just wait for a minute I am coming there Priya" Dhanu hung up the phone and got up from bed. He immediately rushed to the bathroom.

Dhanu went to Priya's room on his bike. He parked bike near gate where Lalitabai was gardening. He did not have time to notice

Lalitabai and he rushed to the Priya's room immediately. Priya was sitting on her bed.

"Hey, Priya are you Okay?' Dhanu asked as he entered in the room.

"Yeah, I am" Priya answered, not moving her eyes from windows.

"Priya what were you saying on the phone?" Dhanu asked, sitting next to Priya.

"I think I am pregnant, I am not sure about it, but I think I am" Priya said.

"Priya, did you get any pregnancy tests done?" Dhanu holds her hand.

"No, that's why I called you Dhanu. I have to do that, but what to do if it is positive" Priya still staring in Dhanu's eyes.

"Nothing yaar, we will talk about it later first get ready and come with me and we will go to the doctor" Dhanu pulled her hand gently.

Priya got ready to go the doctor, she was silent and depressed but Dhanu did not notice it.

Dhanu and Priya went to the doctor for pregnancy tests meanwhile Priya didn't speak much with Dhanu.

After getting tests done they landed in Priya's room again. Priya sat on the cot Dhanu followed her and sat near her "Hey, Priya why are you getting nervous yaar, I am there with you" Dhanu kept his hand on Priya's shoulder.

Priya turned towards Dhanu and cupped his face "That's what I wanted to hear from you Dhanu, it's our child, our first child and we should care for it".

"Don't worry Priya, we will talk to our parents if your reports comes positive, we will definitely search some way for it, and whatever be the results of report I am going to talk with my mother today about you, and about our love" Dhanu said and hugged Priya.

"Oh, I love you Dhanu" Priya liberated herself in Dhanu's embrace.

"Now you just relax and don't panic. Take rest here I will come in the evening after collecting the reports from the doctor, Okay?" Dhanu released her body slowly on the bed.

"Okay, bye" Priya smiled and said goodbye. Dhanu went to his home, he asked Priya to not panic but Dhanu couldn't stop himself from panicking. He was thinking of his orthodox and dominant mother if she knew that Priya is pregnant she will never give permission for their marriage and Dhanu still had no guts for rebelling against his mother.

In the evening Dhanu came to Priya's room. She was lying on the bed with eyes closed. Dhanu sat near her and stared at her face for long time, as Priya sensed something she immediately woke up. It was Dhanu seating near her bed and staring her, "Hey Dhanu when did you came? You should have waked me up" but Dhanu just smiled in response.

"What's that in your hand?" Priya asked pointing towards pages in

Dhanu's hand.

"These are your reports Priya" Dhanu's face was quiet, and eyes were looking miserable. Priya immediately took the report from Dhanu's hand and hastily started reading it and it was clearly stating that Priya was pregnant!

Dhanu kept his hand on Priya's shoulders for condolence but Priya was still staring at the report, two drops of tears rolled down from Priya's eyes "Hey, don't cry baby, everything will be all right" Dhanu pulled her head on his chest.

"I am not crying Dhanu, I am just thinking that I should have thought about my aai, baba before doing that" Priya said while placing that report in it's envelop.

"Hey, why are you thinking like that? Priya look, together we both will tackle this situation. Today itself I am going to talk with my mother about you, firstly I will not talk about this matter because I am scared about her nature she will definitely not accept a child before marriage but I will manage something" said Dhanu.

"What? How could you say just a child before marriage Dhanu, it's our child and we are not toddler's who did this just as an amusement, we did this with our mutual understanding and we are equally responsible for this Dhanu, I don't know about you but I will not lie to anybody because I think I have not done anything wrong" Priya said looking towards Dhanu, her voice becoming firm and strong.

"Okay, okay baba I said na, I will manage something don't be hyper. I will talk to mom today, I am yours Priya and that's the only truth. I know" Dhanu released Priya on the bed and stood up to go. He was trying to comfort Priya with these words but he himself was scared from inside because he had to stand in front of his mother, mother against whom he never spoke a single word in his life, nor had he seen his father doing this. She was completely Orthodox, and despite being a lawyer and a well educated women. She had the thoughts of eighteenth century Indian women for her daughter in law. She was a strict disciplinarian. And most important wass that she hated any person who refused to listen her.

Dhanu went directly to his home. He wanted to speak to his friends very badly but his ego stopped him. When Dhanu reached home, it was around 9:00. He went to the hall and sat on the chair to remove his shoes, "Dhanu you came at the right time. Come for dinner, I have made your favorite dish today" his mother sensed him from the kitchen and invited him for dinner.

Dhanu went to the bathroom to get fresh, he splashed water on his face but his mind was occupied with Priya, he was feeling senseless about the things going around him but body was just following it's routine. He took the towel to dry the face "How was the day son?" his father asked from behind but Dhanu couldn't hear him "I said how was the day Dhanu?" his father asked again but Dhanu was with Priya and he didn't reply.

Dhanu changed and came to the kitchen where his parents were sitting. Dhanu took a chair sat on it "What happened Dhanu?" his father asked looking at him anxiously.

"Nothing great" Dhanu replied while staring at steams coming from the vessel kept on gas.

"Mom, Dad I want to say something to you today" Dhanu initiated still staring at the steams.

"What beta? Is there anything wrong?" mother tried to guess.

"No mom nothing is wrong but this thing I should share with both of you much before"

"What?" Father asked.

"I love a girl in my class and I want to marry her" Dhanu revealed finally what was revolving around in his mind.

"What? Who is that girl?" his mother spluttered in anger.

"You know her and you have seen her with me"

"Is she Priya?" Mother asked?

"Yes"

"No, not at any cost Dhanu, I don't like that girl" Mom gave her decision immediately.

"I knew that you will reply like this, what is the problem in that girl, mom? I have known her for four years she is a good girl" Dhanu stood up in anger and the chair fell down.

"Definitely she must be a good girl but I don't like her and that's all" his Mom's voice became rougher.

"But what's the problem?" Dhanu yelled at her.

"Problem is her modern behavior and her attitude. I want a decent girl for you who should believe in traditional values and she is not that type of girl, I have chosen a girl for you" She had fixed everything by herself she didn't even think of Dhanu's choice and his life because according to her thinking these modern love and affairs are like mushrooms that grow rapidly in rainy season and vanish with the same speed.

"This is not going to happen. Mom you can't do this to me" Dhanu yelled again.

"Bina, at least we should try to consider his choice once. You should go and meet that girl once, after that we can take the decision. Dhanu's father broke his silence and interfered in the matter.

"You don't know these so called modern girls they are just out of control and I want a girl of my choice in my home" Mom spluttered.

""But at least we should give his choice one chance, listen to me, you go to meet her, talk to her and then take a decision and that decision will be final for Dhanu" father said by staring at Dhanu.

"Okay, if you believe it's right, then I will go to meet her but could you make me sure that Dhanu will accept my last decision" mom lastly agreed on father's suggestion.

"Yeah, definitely he will accept it, it will be final decision and it will be good for our family because the girl which will marry with Dhanu has to live with you and me also and it is important that she will be liked by all of us" Dhanu's father passed the bill and turned towards Dhanu now "You will accept na Dhanu?" father asked him and at the moment Dhanu had no choice but to say yes.

"Okay, you go to meet her and then give your decision" Dhanu agreed.

"And in turn you shall meet a girl of my choice" Mom kept new condition in front of him.

Dhanu listened, and went to his room the battle has just cooled down for the day but definitely wasn't resolved yet.

Next day early morning Dhanu's mother went to Priya's room to meet her she didn't take Dhanu with her nor did she inform him that she is going to meet Priya as she knew her room and it was near to Dhanu's home she went alone to meet her future daughter –in-law.

Dhanu's mom reached at the gate of Lalitabai's house, she opened the gate and it made some noise while opening and Lalitabai came out of room to see who's there and she got surprised to see Mrs. Bina coming to her home. Lalita bai and Dhanu's mom were familiar with each other as Lalitabai used to go court frequently for her pending ancient property cases where she had some interactions with Dhanu's mother and thus she was surprised to see her here.

"Oh, Mrs. Kulkarni my goodness welcome, how come you are here?" Lalitabai greeted her and at the same time asked the purpose of her visit.

"Oh, Lalitabai I didn't know that it is your home, I just came to visit a girl I think she stays at your room as a paying guest" Mrs. Kulkarni slowly but not completely revealed her purpose of visit.

"Oh, are you talking about Priya is she your relative?" Lalitabai's facial expression suddenly changed by listening Priya's name and Dhanu's Lawyer mother noticed that.

"No, no Lalitabai, she is relative of my one known person, as she stays near my house. He suggested me to just meet her after all it becomes our duty to help a alone girl leaving away from parents so, I just came to meet her" Dhanu's mom cleverly skipped the matter of her son and Priya's marriage.

"Yes, you are right Mrs. Kulkarni and you know well how today's world is, okay let it be first come to my home and have a cup of tea" Lalitabai invited Mrs. Kulkarni for tea and off course for a chat.

Dhanu's mother sat on a chair in hall and Lalitabai went to the kitchen for making tea, "Lalitabai, just half a cup. I don't take much tea you know".

"Don't worry Mrs. Kulkarni I also avoid tea but it is good to have it once in a while" Lalitabai added with her patented fake smile.

"How is that girl Lalitabai?, I mean you know how today's modern girls are so I just asked you" Dhanu's mother came directly on the business.

"Oh, thanks god Mrs. Kulkarni you asked it from your side I was wondering how to say it to you" Lalitabai took a long breath kept a cup aside on table and prepared herself to start her favorite business 'gossiping'.

"Is there anything Lalitabai?" Dhanu's mother asked with scared face.

"Yes, Mrs. Kulkarni, that girls behavior is not so good, I mean her contacts with the boys, her twenty four hour hanging out with the boys, late night comings, oh terrible, I tell you Mrs. Kulkarni if I had such a daughter I would have definitely killed her and also hanged myself after that" Lalitabai stopped finally to take a breath, after all she got some one after long time to speak on Priya.

Dhanu's mother was shocked to hear these heartbreaking sentences about her son's choice and her future daughter – in – law but Lalitabai wasn't finished yet.

"This is nothing Mrs. Kulkarni one early morning I saw a boy coming out of her room, I tried to see him but he escaped rapidly, no doubt he had spent the night with her" Lalitabai mumbled, taking her face near to Mrs. Kulkarni's ears in a fashion that no one could listen.

"This is all shocking Lalitabai. Are you hundred percent sure of your words? I am asking because I learned that she is very good girl" Mrs. Kulkarni tried to assure about Priya again.

"What could a widow like me achieve by saying false words about someone, it is all pure truth and nothing else. I can swear by any god" Lalitabai now started to try hard to prove her truthfulness, she dragged god in the matter.

"It is not that I never warned her or never told her that she is going by the wrong path but you know these girls, she started to blame me. She is so arrogant you know, she never listens to elders and she also insulted me. From that day I left that business. If her parents themselves are not bothered about her then why should I?" Lalitabai now perfectly did her job of bowing seeds of abhorrence in Mrs. Kulkarni's mind about Priya.

Mrs. Kulkarni was completely shocked. The cup was untouched and she was continuously staring at Lalitabai counting her rapidly changing facial expressions.

"You are not saying anything Mrs. Kulkarni" Lalitabai asked.

"Umm... what is there to say Lalitabai. Today's generation is like this and girls staying away from home are big worry for parents" Mrs. Kulkarni muttered with tensed facial expressions.

"Yes, you are right but parents are also responsible for this they should at least come to see what their child is doing how could one blindly rely on such an arrogant girl" Lalitabai added.

"Leave it Lalitabai, what could you and me do in this matter. Let her live her own life with her own principles, Okay now I think I must take your permission it's too late" Mrs. Kulkarni stood up from chair.

"Oh, you are leaving Mrs. Kulkarni? You wanted to see Priya na?" Lalitabai inquired.

"No, its too late Lalitabai I have to go to court, I should leave"

Mrs. Kulkarni prepared herself to leave .

"Okay, come some another day we will have a chat, now you know my house " Lalitabai gave invitation for next visit.

"Yeah, definitely" Mrs. Kulkarni knew that it would be impossible for her to come here again but despite that she promised with a fake smile on face.

Dhanu's mother left Lalitabai's house and matter of Priya started revolving in her mind with high intensity, her feet were moving fast towards home and her mind was burying herself in a deep sorrow, she was feeling bruised, trodden and scared for her only son's future.

She came in front a gate of her house and felt something strange she loosed her control on self, her hands were shivering, and heartbeat increased rapidly her whole body is sweating like never before and suddenly she lost her control and fell unconscious on ground Dhanu's father was doing some gardening at their backyard, he heard some strange sound and was shocked to see his wife unconscious on the ground.

He immediately called Dhanu who was in the hall of their home. They both lifted her in hands and taken her into home, Dhanu anxiously called an ambulance to take his mother to hospital he knew that his mother had B.P. problem but this type of incident happened for the very first time with them, his father was speechless, after a few tense minutes, the ambulance reached their home. The hospital staff rushed in to find the patient. They put her on a stretcher and took towards ambulance, Dhanu and his father followed them. In ambulance stature was placed at the middle position of the backseats of ambulance, father – son seated on either sides of the patient, Dhanu's father was holding her hand and staring at her face tensely with moist eyes and Dhanu felt broken at the moment.

Dhanu was sitting against the bed of his mother in ICU, staring to the saline bottle, doctors has said that she had had a mild heart attack but now she was out of the danger. This incident pulled the whole Kulkarni family in tension, Dhanu was waiting for his mother to become conscious so that he could speak to her to know whether there was anything which is worrying her deeply. Doctors strictly warned him that she should never be given any emotional shock till she recovers from her illness Dhanu's father was sitting outside the ICU in the waiting area with a tense face.

And at one moment mother awoke, her eyes opened slowly and she delighted to see Dhanu sitting near her "Dhanu beta,.." Mrs. Kulkarni murmured taking her hand to Dhanu's face.

"Yes, mom I am here, near you" Dhanu assured his presence to her.

"You are all right mom, nothing has happened to you"

"I know my son" she placed her hand on her head in blessing.

"I will call papa, you just wait mom" Dhanu moved to call his father.

"Wait beta" Dhanu's mother held his hand to stop him Dhanu sat again on the chair he asked with low voice "What mom?"

"Beta I want one promise from you, will you do one thing for me?"

"Promise? Say mom what's that"

"Beta promise me today, no swear by me that you will not marry that girl Priya"

"What mom?" Dhanu reiterated stunningly.

"Take my swear beta you will never take again that girl's name in our home" One more fireball from Mom and Dhanu was speechless.

"Mom we will talk about it later first you get well, and come to home soon nothing is more important than you for us" Dhanu tried well to tackle the situation.

"No I will not hear anything from you Dhanu, promise me otherwise I will never talk to you and your father" Mother used her last and final weapon and Dhanu was obliterated, he remembered Doctors words that a tiny shock to her mother may lead to worse condition.

"Okay, mom I will not marry her, I will not marry her until you say so, I will not take her name in front of you, in front of dad, in front of anybody not even myself that's my promise mom" Dhanu promised with void mind, he was destroyed from inside but had to look happy for his mother. He has to scarify his love for the one who showed him this world and for the one who scarified her happiness of life for his wellbeing.

Dhanu promised and suddenly woke up from the chair he ran

towards the door of ICU, his father was seating on the bench in waiting area in front of ICU. "Papa, mom is awake" these words were sufficient his father rose from chair and rushed towards ICU, Dhanu went to the bathroom to wash his face and necessarily to washout emotions which could be clearly seen on his face.

Dhanu sat in the waiting area of ICU for some time. After four hours he got time to relax in the chair, he remembered his mobile which he had put on silent mode while entering in ICU, it had 8 missed calls from Priya. Dhanu sprang into anxiety seeing those missed calls, who should be given more importance in such a situation loving girlfriend who is carrying your baby or caring mother who is in ICU just because of you. Damn difficult question. I am sure no one could answer it! What a dilemma!.

Dhanu got the blues, he never faced life with bare foot alone, he always had friends like me and Abhi with him and now walking with barefoot in life's hard blaze was prickling for him.

Dhanu thought something in his mind and pressed Abhi's number "Hey, Dhanu how are you my friend?" Abhi asked from other side.

"Abhi, I need you yaar, actually I need you both you and Mit"

"What happened Dhanu?, everything is alright?"

"Come here Abhi, we will talk, I am at city hospital"

"City hospital? What's the matter Dhanu?' Abhi inquired.

"Come here I will tell you everything Abhi"

"Okay, be there I am on the way" Abhi hung up the phone saying this.

Abhi reached at city hospital in couple of minutes and he easily discovered Dhanu sitting lonely at ICU waiting area.

"Who is in the ICU Dhanu?" Abhi asked impatiently.

"My mom"

"What? And you are telling me now" Abhi stunned.

"Sorry Abhi but situation was like that, I was not in the condition to contact anyone, Okay let's go to canteen. I need a cup of tea" Dhanu stood up to go to the hospital canteen.

"What happened Dhanu?" Abhi reiterated the question while sitting in the chair at hospital canteen.

"A mild heart attack, Doctors saying she is out of danger now" Dhanu answered and drunk water kept on the table hastily.

""Did you inform Priya?"

"No"

"Why?"

"Because I didn't find it necessary" Dhanu said peevishly.

"Is there anything wrong Dhanu?" Abhi asked silently.

"Wrong, yes everything is going wrong Abhi and that can't be ever corrected. Things have gone so bad, did you know the reason of that heart attack to my mom? It's me, it's only me and now she wants me to never take the name of Priya. She hates Priya, Abhi, and now she will never allow me to marry her." Dhanu broken into the tears, he put his head on the table and cried silently.

"Abhi sat on the chair beside Dhanu and kept his hand on Dhanu's shoulders "Hey, everything will be alright buddy let your mom get well soon and then we will talk to her" Abhi offered condole.

"No, not at all Abhi, I promised my mom that I will never see her face, and I have decided to do so" Dhanu said wiping his tears.

"Are you kidding Dhanu? It's not that easy and this is not the wise way to handle the dilemma. Please don't overreact" Abhi said, stunned.

"I am not overreacting Abhi, I have seen my mom fighting for her life in the ICU, there is no doubt I love Priya but my mom is more important for me and I have decided to act as per her will and if she thinks that I should not meet Priya then I will not" Abhi said firmly

"You are in the shock Dhanu, we will talk later" Abhi moved to stand up from the chair and suddenly Dhanu's mobile rang he saw it was Priya and he switched of the Phone.

"Don't do this to that girl Dhanu" Abhi mumbled.

"I am doing it willfully Abhi you don't know the criticality of the situation, come with me" Dhanu woke up and started to climb stairs to go to the terrace of the hospital, Abhi followed him.

They reached at the hospital terrace where one could see the whole city, the rush of peoples but no sound a near about silence Dhanu stopped near one corner and started to speak looking at the infinity.

"Abhi, Priya is carrying my child" Dhanu said with a blank face.

"What?" this is ultimate surprise for Abhi and he registered the only reaction.

"And I think we should break off our relation as soon as possible now, before it's too late" Dhanu still not looking at Abhi's face.

"I never ever thought that you will do this to the girl who loved you most, who just thought of you every time, who gave her everything to you, Don't do this Dhanu! You both will suffer from this"

"Then what should I do Abhi? I tried my level best to convince my mother, but things have gone worse, and this is the situation when I hadn't told her about Priya's pregnancy, did you think that she will be happily convinced about this marriage after knowing the truth, no way I know my mother well, I will tell everything to Priya later. I will convince her" Dhanu said looking at the ground.

"What will you tell her?"

"I will tell her to abort the child" now Dhanu looked at Abhi's face

"You are sick Dhanu, you have turned into a basket case, do whatever with your life but don't play this bad game with that innocent girl for god's sake" Abhi yelled at Dhanu peevishly.

"What? You are cursing me? I thought you will help me in this situation and you are going on cursing me" Dhanu shouted back.

"Yes you are cursed, and no one can help you, you made yourself into a monster Dhanu, go to the hell" Abhi started to walk away from Dhanu in anger.

"Yes, go away you were never my, go away I don't need anyone" Dhanu shouted and kept on shouting till Abhi vanished from his eyesight.

11
DARK TIMES

Abhi reached his room with heavy heart and teary eyes, he opened the room's door and sat at the corner looking towards the infinity, his body was shivering, he forget to switch on the lights of his room. All the thoughts were thundering in his mind at the same time. He was feeling like a stupid, dumb person who cannot do anything while situation was getting worse in front of him he was feeling cursed, and believe me friends, this is no worse feeling someone can have, when you knows something is going wrong in front of you and the circumstances need you, no, they are shouting with all the energy to call you to hinder, but you are hemmed in and you can do nothing but cursing yourself with countless words, and Abhi was now in the same dilemma.

Abhi suddenly shook up by the mobile ringing. It was Priya, he picked up the phone "Yeah Priya" Abhi said with unusual low voice.

"Abhi what's up?"

"Nothing great, you say where you are yaar"

"In my room only"

"Okay and Dhanu?" Abhi asked to show that he is unaware of everything.

"Yeah, I don't know even I called you to ask where is he, his mobile is switched off"

"Yeah, Priya he might be busy in some work, don't worry about him"

"Abhi I think I should go to his home to see everything is okay"

"Oh, don't do that Priya, there is no need at all. You girls are so possessive yaar but you know guys sometimes need a little bit space, he might be busy in work. Don't worry he will call you and if there is any problem don't hesitate to call me at any time" Abhi gave her a false picture of the situation.

"Okay, Abhi I think you are right. I was unnecessarily worried, okay goodnight take care"

"Good night, Priya" Abhi hung up the phone and tears rolled down from his eyes, so frightened he was feeling at the moment, he was feeling cursed.

Suddenly, the door of the room opened Abhi looked in that direction, he saw Gulab coming from college. "Hey buddy why are you seating in dark, lights are gone or what?"

"No yaar, just thinking on the bloody games that life is playing with us"

"Hey, dude be aware you are turning philosopher and it's harmful for your image" Gulab bantered.

Abhi chuckled and wiped his tears slowly, "Hey, Gulab what's your plan now?"

"Nothing"

"Then let's go"

"Where?"

"Anna's dhaba" Abhi muttered.

"Oh, I guess something is wrong, fine let's go 'Khushi aur gum dono ka saathi Rum'"

Abhi and Gulab finally landed at their favorite destination – 'Anna's dhaba'.

Here In Ahmedabad I got a call of Abhi when I was in the way to my room "Hey, Abs what's up bro" I greeted in fervent voice.

"Hey, Mit missing you a lot man" Abhi replied in low frequency which is sufficient for me to know that he is drunk.

"Hey, is there a party Abhi who is with you?"

"No one, no one my friend I am alone and first time in life I am feeling this bloody loneliness"

"Hey, Abhi tell me, what happened?" I sensed something wrong.

And Abhi told me everything he got to know from Dhanu, everything that happened between Dhanu and Priya and regarding every pain that their relationship was suffering from.

It hurt me a lot. My eyes become moist hands started to shiver without knowledge of my mind I felt like someone was drilling my heart with a drilling machine.

"Is Priya aware of everything?" I inquired.

"Not yet"

"Okay, then go to her"

'What?"

"I said go to her or call her at a common place tell her everything going around her, tell her what's there in Dhanu's mind and then call Dhanu there" I suggested my way to resolve the crisis.

"But, then what will she think of me, she might misunderstand me and Dhanu? What will he think?" Abhi grew flustered.

"Don't be selfish Abhi your image is not important than Priya's life go and tell her everything and convince Dhanu that he is wrong" I reiterated.

"Okay, if you think it is right then I will do it, I will call both of them tomorrow morning at my room's terrace"

"Fine, but don't tell Dhanu that Priya is coming otherwise he will never come, he is not having guts to face the reality and don't worry about Priya she is a strong girl and I think Dhanu will get easily convinced in her presence" I reassured him that things will be okay.

"Then what about his mother?"

"We have to wait for that let come from hospital, we all will go to her"

"Yaar Mit thanks yaar, you just solved the crisis in minutes and I am drinking this fucking Rum in tension" Abhi got some relief

"Doesn't matter friend, don't forget to tell me everything tomorrow"

Our discussion ended with a sought of relief but matter hasn't resolved still tomorrows day is waiting for us. And we never knew that it will be a judgment day for Priya and Dhanu's relation.

Next day morning Abhi did his work sincerely he called Priya at his room at 9:00 AM. And Priya came on time thus first step of the plan ended with success now remains the second step of successfully telling Priya about a crisis happening in Dhanu's life.

Abhi saw Priya from terrace and asked to come there directly, priya appeared there with her decent smile, she was looking stunning in sky blue salwar kameez.

"This is the first time in this month you are coming to my room Priya" Abhi initiated.

"Yeah, long time after Mit's leaving Mumbai we hadn't done any get together, Okay leave that I came today just to meet you as soon as you called that's important, tell me,anything new now a days?"

"Yeah life seems to be taking some new turns" said Abhi while relaxing to the wall.

"Hey, listen Abhi I want to confess something to you, I and Dhanu hid one thing from you and Mit actually we didn't get an opprtune time to tell all this stuff to you but you both deserve to share this" says Priya interrupted.

"I know Priya" Abhi interrupted.

"What? How?" Priya asked.

"Dhanu told me"

"Oh, then you knew it ha!"

"And I want to tell you something more"

"What's that?"

"Priya, Dhanu told his mom about your relationship and he also confessed that he wants to marry you"

"Yes? But how come he hasn't told it to me" Priya interrupted.

"Listen Priya, listen very carefully, Dhanu's mom was extremely upset after that I don't know what happened exactly in between but she got a mild heart attack and she was admitted in the hospital" Abhi finished his avowal and glanced towards Priya.

"What! Things gone that bad and Dhanu didn't think it was necessary to at least inform me" Priya sat down in shock.

"Look Priya he might be baffled, he couldn't handle the situation but wait for some time, time is a best medicine we will talk to his mom and everything will be Okay" Abhi tried to clarify Dhanu's side.

"No, Abhi nothing is going to be okay, if Dhanu has bothered about his mother then I am also nervous for the child in my stomach, is this commitment? Didn't he know from beginning that he has to tackle this situation at one point of our relationship?" Priya was right. She was preparing her mind setup for these expected obstacles in the path of their love, the path which was chosen by both of them with mutual understanding and awareness of future dissents by their own parents.

Abhi was still having a hope or he had no other choice rather than relying on the defeated and crushed Dhanu in the hope that his mind will change and he will also understand Priya's pain.

"Priya, let's finish this crisis I am going to call Dhanu here, I will ask him for his final answer and I want you there" Abhi took his mobile to call Dhanu, he looked at Priya for any response but she didn't replied and didn't looked at what he is going to do, she was not concerned about the things going around her now she was looking at the infinity with the blank mind.

Abhi called Dhanu and this time Dhanu picked up phone

"Hi, Abhi"

"Hi Dhanu how is your mom now?"

"yeah, she is fine Doctors are saying she will be discharged soon"

"Nice it's great news that means your tension is relieved"

"Yeah, you can say like that, and one more thing Abhi I am sorry for that day's behavior Abhi, I was totally out of control"

"It's okay Dhanu I can understand, Dhanu if you are free right now can you manage to come to my room?"

"yes, I can yaar, I am coming in five minutes"

"Fine, I am here on terrace come directly here"

"Okay, I am leaving"

Abhi disconnected the mobile and looked at Priya "You didn't tell him that I am here?"

"No, I did not"

"Why?"

"Because I was scared , that he will refuse to come"

"Then let him do that why did you lie to him?"

"Look Priya I want to make up your relation at any cost, and for that it is very necessary that you and Dhanu should talk face to face"

"Don't do this much for me Abhi, If it is written in our destiny, then no one can change it no one can change his fate Abhi" Priya's eyes turned moist.

"Hey, Priya I can't believe that a girl like you can accept her defeat easily by cursing her fate, don't let that Priya get lost which I always seen in you" Abhi come near to Priya and wiped her tears which could have rolled down from her eyes at any moment.

"Thanks Abhi"

"Priya go first and wash your face, look at your face I don't want you to meet Dhanu with such a sad face"

"Okay" Priya went towards the bathroom for getting fresh and Abhi quite relaxed as his plan was going the right way.

After a moment Dhanu came on his bike Abhi signaled him from terrace to come there.

"I am waiting for you Dhanu, how are you?" Abhi greeted him by hugging.

"It's Okay Abhi, mom is good but some things gone worse for lifetime" said Dhanu going away from Abhi.

"Are talking about Priya?" Abhi inquired.

"Yes Abhi, I cheated her; I can't ever give a justice to her" Said Dhanu with nuisance.

"I have called you here to talk about her only"

"Sorry, Abhi please leave that matter I feel lost on that subject" Dhanu said peevishly.

"What? Now she is just a subject for you, how can you be so cheap Dhanu and for a girl who has given her everything to you and trusted you more than herself"

"Yes, I loved her, she trusted me the most but now my priority is my family; my mother, who given me birth, who raised me by feeding her milk, what can I do Abhi tell me" Dhanu grew more frustrated.

"Yeah, you are bothered about a mother who gave birth to you and what about your child which she will deliver" Abhi almost shouted at him.

"Don't make me more flustered Abhi, I want to put her out of my mind, I want to forget everything now, I can't move that relation to the end" Dhanu threw away his every blame.

Priya was listening that conversation from behind, she was speechless she was ditched by the person whom she loved most and not even informed her.

"So, now I remain just a subject for you, who you want to forget now" said Priya from the behind with her voice shivering.

Dhanu looked back stunned, he had never thought that Priya will be present here, "priya..you are…"

"Yes, I am here, I came here before you, thanks Abhi for not telling him that I am here otherwise how will I come to know how cheap he is" Priya busted on Dhanu.

"Oh, Abhi it's your planning, you cheated me, you called me here just to trap me and I was thinking that you are my true friend" Dhanu started blaming Abhi without responding to Priya.

"Stop blaming others Dhanu, you are a looser, you are acting like hypocrite. What about all that promises you made to me why did you cheat me Dhanu, talk to me, tell to me why did you do this to me?, why? Answer me Dhanu" Priya collapsed on the knees her palms kissed the floor she looked boneless, feeble like never before, tears fell down from her eyes and touched floor but still Dhanu's heart was not going to melt for her,

"Yes, I am a looser, I am a damn looser, I am a hypocrite I can't stand pressure. I rationalize from the truth, Okay I accept, I accept everything now you are happy, but Priya now I can't leave my family in hell just for the sake of my happiness and I don't have the guts to fight with the world for my love and please for the heaven's sake leave me alone" Dhanu blasted. He just broke all the relations in one sentence, he hurt Priya for life time and now he moved to walk out from that place.

Abhi, who was silently watching all this muddle become active as soon as Dhanu moved towards the stairs, he obstructed Dhanu's way by standing in front of him"Stop Dhanu, you can't go like this" Abhi shouted.

"oh, who are you to stop me Abhi, don't interfere in our matter" Dhanu spluttered back.

"I am her friend and it's my duty to protect her, and I can go to any stage to do that" Abhi's tone became rough, his eyes fired with the anger.

"Oh, now she is your friend, then do whatever you want but I am not going to stay here" Dhanu chucked Abhi's hand away from his body.

"Stop Dhanu, what about your baby, what will that lonely girl do? Try to think Dhanu" Abhi insisted for last.

"I have suggested Abhi, I am also helpless there is no other option except abortion" Dhanu mumbled with low frequency.

"What? What are talking about Dhanu, how dare you again utter this" Abhi give him a mild push.

"Wait Abhi let him go, let him live his own life, I was wrong. I counted on a wrong person, I will not be his obstacle from now onwards" now Priya had aroused herself from the shock and she firmly stood up against Dhanu.

"Priya, this is bloody cheating yaar he can't leave you like this" Abhi murmured with a broken voice

"Let him do that Abhi I don't want to beg in front of such a loafer, I will find my own way" Priya uttered.

"Go Dhanu what a looser you are, I feel pity for you, you lost a girl like Priya shame on your life" Abhi pushed him hard but this time Dhanu did not protest, he found his way and left the place hastily. He did not wait for a moment, he left nothing back he had finished the friendship of years in minutes he broke relations of lifetime in seconds.

Abhi dropped Priya at her room after some time both were speechless one kind of silence was existing between them. Priya was still in a shock and Abhi was unable to discover words to initiate.

"Okay, Abhi.." Priya said while moving towards gate and Abhi moved his bike.

"Abhi, just a minute" Priya called from back.

"Yes, Priya"

"Abhi I have decided to go home by tomorrow morning bus"

"Okay, but when will you come back"

"I don't know, will you manage to come to drop me"

"Fine I will be here by 8:00, is it Okay?"

"Okay"Said priya and moved towards stairs.

Abhi left that place with a distracted mind. He wanted to calm the storm of thoughts thundering in his mind, so Abhi took his bike towards 'college katta' , not just a spot it could be referred as a holy place of our friendship where our friendship was nurtured, cherished and grown to its height.

Where we four friends shared our feelings with each other, where we came closer to each other's hearts, and where we promised ourselves to not leave each other alone. And now the wheel of destiny took us to the turn where there was nothing, there was simply nothing which could ever be referred to as a friendship.

Someone has said very well 'Nothing is Permanent'

But I never thought Friendship also comes in that category, but yes now with a gloomy heart, I am obligated to say yes, friendship also comes in the category of temporary stuff, definitely friendship is an eternal blessing and I am very tiny being to deny this Universal truth but human being is susceptible to change, he is used to flow with the direction of his interest and here he can even spoil such holy relations for his benefits.

Abhi remained there for two to three hours sitting alone with tumbling wind and twinkling stars. After that he left the place but this Abhi was different he is no more that old Abhi. Something had changed him absolutely and he was now ready to live with that change.

12
PRIYA GOES HOME

Next day morning Abhi went to Priya's room to pick up her, he called Priya from outside she was ready to go and just waiting for Abhi to come.

"Coming Abhi" Priya answered.

Abhi preferred to wait outside Lalitabai is doing some her routine work she noticed Abhi and attempted to catch his eye (god knows for what purpose), but Abhi ignored her and stood there calmly.

He looked at the Priya's door when it made a sound while opening. Priya come out carrying a bag in one hand, Abhi looked at her once and his eyes paused over her face "Oh, my god is this a same Priya whom I used to know" Abhi murmured to himself.

Priya was coming down the stairs with a tranquil face. She was looking different, not the same Priya who we used to meet every day, definitely we missed that bubbly, naughty but still caring Priya.

Abhi caught himself feeling guilty as he thought that he was responsible for all this. He induced Dhanu to propose Priya, he let all this happened between them but now, he was helpless, he could not change whatever had happened the only thing he could ever do was to remain her friend forever.

Priya sat on the bike quietly, no one said anything, but how could Lalitabai control her curiosities she come forward and asked "Are you going home Priya?"

"Yes, Lalitabai I am going to my home for some days but I will be back"

"Okay, no problem beta I was just asking for the information" Lalitabai offered fake smile to Priya.

On bus stand, Priya got the bus going to Pune and sat on the window seat, Abhi was standing outside sitting on his bike. He had done his job of dropping Priya to bus stand and he could go if he wished so but something was not permitting him to go before Priya's bus left the stand. Priya was busy on mobile checking something and Abhi was pretending to be busy by attempting to read the Advertisement at the corner of Bus stand.

"Abhi, you may leave now there is some more time for Bus to leave" Priya breaks the silence.

"Doesn't matter Priya. I am fine here, I will wait till your Bus starts" Abhi tried to become diplomatic.

"Okay, then..." Priya was trying to collect the words for

conversation but found herself unable and kept quite.

"Priya I will buy some fruit for you" Abhi went to the fruit stall without waiting for Priya's response.

He brought some fruits for Priya and here fruits became just a measure to fill the gap of words to pass the time, he passed the fruits to Priya and Bus started Priya waved her hand to say bye, and all the thoughts which were blocked at some place of his mind started to thunder suddenly. Priya was leaving and he had so many things to ask her, he didn't even assured her that he was with her at any cost, and he still hadn't said sorry to her if she thought he was responsible for the mess. But the time had gone now Bus was taking a turn and it would look silly if he ran behind the Bus, Abhi stood over there for some time looking at the dust spread in environment due to the Bus.

Priya went to her home town to meet parents, and here Dhanu's mom returned from hospital, she became well and started a very important work of her searching a bride for her only son. She started searching for a girl for Dhanu in her relations and at their native place. She didn't want to take a chance this time she wanted to engage her son as soon as possible.

Dhanu was totally aware of everything going on at his home about his marriage but he was ignoring the fact, maybe he was not interested even in knowing that what his was mom planning for his marriage. He had surrendered his body, soul and even his feelings to his mom, and now he was just ready to flow with what will be happening

around him.

Abhi told me the situation over phone, I tried Dhanu for hundreds of times but he used to avoid my calls also and at last I decided to go to Mumbai, I had to do whatever I can do for Priya and of course for Dhanu.

It was 15th November 2005, great month of winter; I alighted at the station and surprised to see the Dracula 'Abhi' waiting for me with the decent smile, "welcome Mit" he greeted me with a hug, but something was missing there, I was missing Abhi's typical warm welcome he seemed mature now.

"So, dude what's up? How's life" I asked, holding his shoulders.

"Nothing yaar, but was missing you" he answered and quickly picked my bag, and we reached my home after taking dinner at my home we landed at 'college katta'.

Abhi landed his butt on katta and immediately blazed a ciggy, "Want a puff?"

"Yeah, you first"

"So tell me Abhi what to do now" I came to the point.

"My mind has been frozen Mit. Priya's innocent face doesn't goes away from my eyesight, you say what to do" Abhi released a ring of smoke in the air.

"Speaking very honestly friend we are no one to do anything in this matter, result of this matter totally depends upon them, what we can do is just we can try to show them a right way but it depends upon them how to tackle this relationship tragedy" I knew that I was being somewhat hard while speaking about my dearest friends but sometimes in life you have to be hard to accept the bitter truth and now it's true that their relationship had some hard to repair damages.

"How can you just say that Mit? Is it Priya's fault? Why should she suffer from this" Abhi spluttered. I was seeing him so possessive about someone, for the first time.

"Don't take it wrong Abhi, but after marriage with Dhanu Priya is not going to live with just Dhanu alone. She has to live with his mother also and for that she should be acceptable to her also. Don't you think that her life will become hell if she couldn't adjust with these new relations" I expressed my self but now there was no reply from Abhi.

"Look Abhi, I want to see Priya happy again, I want to see that same bubbly Priya again, and it will not be possible if she compromises with life, she cannot live happily with the someone who has ditched her when she needed him most, she cannot be happy with someone who had smashed her faith" I was speaking and Abhi was looking in my eyes cigarette had become a essence stick in between us.

"You might be right, Mit, but I think we should try for the last time you should talk with Dhanu" Abhi insisted.

"Yes, you are right Abhi, I will, rather my purpose of coming is that only I will speak not only with Dhanu but with his mom also" I made my final statement and smashed the useless cigarette.

"What? You are going to meet his mom?" Abhi asked, surprised.

"Yes, I will try to convince her"

"Be careful Mit she is a heart patient" Abhi insisted but I knew it and I knew her nature also very well, so I was sure that I would be a good diplomat.

13
MEETING DHANU'S MOM

I planned meeting Dhanu's mom next morning and I managed to find a time when Dhanu would not be at home, this was just to avoid Dhanu's interruptions or you may say his anxiousness which will strike him for sure when he will see his dear friend speaking to his heart patient mother about the matter which will definitely send his mother again to the hospital with another heart attack, so I reached the place at preplanned time in a preplanned manner, taking some fruits with me for aunty.

"Good morning aunty" I greeted her with smile when she opened the door.

"Oh, Mit beta after a long time, beta please come in" she welcomed me at home I entered and sat on the chair, putting the bag of fruits on the table first, TV was on and aunty seemed to be watching some saas bahu kind of program. I always wonder how ladies can tolerate this kind of nonsense and purely meaningless serials running on some channels, but here they not only watch it but these are their favorite programs. They can forget to have a meal but not watching their favorite serial. God please save them and lead them to the right path!, Okay leave it this is not my concern I came here to solve Dhanu-Priya's love tragedy.

"I am making tea for you Mit" Aunty said from kitchen.

Tea, my favorite drink and how can I say no to tea yaar so I said "yeah sure Aunty"

Two steamy cups came from the kitchen and landed on the table. Smell of hot tea stimulated my nervous system and I become somewhat fearless to tackle the situation.

"Say beta what's going on? How is your mom?" Mother Dhanu asked about Mother Mit.

"Yeah, she is all right aunty but I heard about you that's why I came to see you how are you now?" I referred to her heart attack.

"What to tell you beta, God has saved me and my family otherwise don't know what would have happened" Aunty sat on sofa in front of me.

"Don't worry Aunty everything will be just all right, just relax and stay cool always" I did the job which most of the people do with patients, giving advice.

"You know my nature very well son, I can't stay cool and now I can't relax until I find a bride for Dhanu" Aunty herself brought up the topic which I am trying to start, Okay Mr. Mit it's time to get started.

"Oh, Aunty you are really searching a bride for Dhanu, I mean, are you serious about that?" I asked, acting surprised.

"Of course beta, after an incident like that I had to do this after all a mother has to think about her child and I know my Dhanu he will never go beyond my words" Eh, and here I find something.

"What kind of Incident Aunty?" I asked with innocent face.

"Don't ask beta, you know that girl studying with Dhanu"

"Which girl you are talking about Aunty?" I became more innocent.

"That what's her name ..yes Priya! That girl did some magic on my son, but god is great he showed me real face of that girl and we saved our Dhanu's life and our Dhanu is now out of all this and listening to me obediently" A mothers heart really cares about her child and we cannot really, we can't blame her for all that happened, oh god if I ever had blamed her for her rudeness and selfish behavior then please forgive me it's not she who is acting like that it's a mothers heart whose love and care make made her selfish for her child's wellness, I was quite for a while so she asked me "What's happen Mit what are you thinking?, did you know that girl?" She enquired looking at my tensed face.

"Yes aunty I know that girl" I answered with quite relax and silent voice

"Then are you aware of Dhanu and her affair?" now she enquired with tensed face.

"Yes" again a shocking answer

And a pin drop silence engulfed us; I saw her face asking me why? Then why you didn't stop my son? But I had to explain, now I had to clean up her mind, now it was my turn.

"Aunty it's not like that. Whatever impression is in your mind is totally wrong. I don't know who made that and what you got to know about Priya but I can say only one thing, she is a good girl Aunty. I know her" I finished whatever I wanted to say for which I planned this visit and stopped suddenly for Aunty's reaction but there was a pin drop silence again. Aunty was staring at me constantly with a blunt face, no reaction at all.

"Look Mit, I don't know much about that girl and I even don't want to know that and I don't wanted to hear her name anymore in this house. I will make the choice for my son. I want a housewife and traditional girl for my son and I have made my choice so please Mit it is better to drop that subject" Aunties mood changed suddenly. I noticed a tremor in her voice and realized that she felt bad but this was a last chance for me. I have to do something now.

"Aunty don't get angry just try to listen me once. Dhanu is like a brother for me and I know his feelings well, you made your choice but what about your son's choice? Why should he spend his entire life with a girl who he does not love, think over it Aunty" I really collected lots of guts to say all this, I know I deserve bravery award or a big slap for this because I am indirectly bothering my friends heart patient mother for a reason for which she got hospitalized some days ago.

"Enough Mit! I never thought you can go to this level. You came here to threaten my mom" A loud, angry voice came up from behind and I suddenly turned to see and my reaction was "Shit…" It was Dhanu and he had heard our conversation.

"Dhanu, she is like my mother too. I care for her as much as you and I know what I am doing very well. I am doing this for you only, you should at least convince her for Priya" I am a pretty good defender I know that.

"I don't want to listen your stupid excuses Mit, why don't you people understand I don't want to marry that girl, I don't like her now please for god sake get out of here and leave us alone" Dhanu shouted at me with anger this time. I was seeing a totally different Dhanu. He had changed, he definitely had changed. He insulted me, I was never treated like this in my life but still I will not blame him for all this. I felt pity for him, poor guy he didn't know where he was leading his life by ignoring true love.

I turned towards Aunty. She was burning with anger, her hands were shivering and I got a signal that I should leave the place, I stood up slowly and moved towards the door. I was speechless, this time this good defender surrendered himself, Dhanu was standing at the door he gave me the way to pass by moving aside slightly, I walked four to five steps towards main gate and looked back towards Dhanu

"I am sorry Priya you are right, this fellow doesn't deserves you at all' I mumbled to myself and left the place.

"I already told you to not to go to that devil's house but why should you listen to Abhi, why the great philosopher Mr. Maitreya will listen to this brainless fellow" Abhi blustered with the anger and I was the only target, because in his view I insulted myself by going there now Dhanu will be on a high, but in my view this was not the matter of high or low nor even of insult or admiration. This was a matter of some one's life and for that these types of insults doesn't matters.

"Look Abhi, leave that subject. Now these things don't matters at all. After all he is our friend he will come on the right path one day for sure" I replied.

"Oh, one day and when will that day come Mr. Mit?" Abhi questioned sarcastically.

"I don't know but for this moment we have to think about Priya only, she is pregnant yaar and she is at her home. Did you have a talk with her? How is she?" I expressed my worry.

"Yeah I talked to her.." Abhi said and suddenly my cell rang. It was Priya, I looked at Abhi with question on my face "Did you tell her about that Dhanu's incident?"

"Ah..umm.. Yeah I told her actually" Abhi started to find words to give explanation but never needed it I picked up the phone.

"Mit...How are you?" sweet voice came from the opposite side.

"I am fine Priya; tell me after such a long time you called me didn't you miss this poor friend"

"I am sorry Mit, it's not like that"

"Okay, Okay leave it yaar, tell me how are you?"

"I am okay, and now I am three months pregnant Mit" Priya said slowly, but this sentence made a hole in my heart.

"What you have you decided Priya?" I asked anxiously.

"Nothing, I am coming there tomorrow"

"Did you...have you told ….. your parents?" I asked her.

"No, Mit I didn't have the guts. I am scared. I don't know what to do. I need to talk to you people"

"Hey, silly girl don't worry at all we are here for you. Tell me when you will come to Mumbai"

"Tomorrow morning at around eleven"

"Okay, done we will be there and listen I am leaving tomorrow night, my train is at eight so we will have fun in the evening okay, till then chill out"

"Okay Mit bye"

"Bye Priya"

"Oh, you devil, you are leaving tomorrow, bloody fool then why didn't you tell me?" Abhi got one more point to shout on me.

"I just forgot it Abhi, but what matters yaar we will have a decent get together in the evening so chill out and lets go" I stood up to go and removed dust from my ass.

"Hey, just wait Mit, she didn't asked you about that incident?" Abhi enquired with surprised face.

"Because she is not a bimbo like you fool, she knew that there will be no result"

"How girls can know everything without speaking a single word yaar" Abhi mumbled to himself and we left the place.

14
PLANS OF DESTINY

Next day morning Abhi and I reached the Bus station on exact time "I just hate this smell yaar" Abhi said irritated.

"Sorry buddy this is India, and this is typical Indian Bus stand" I mocked him.

"But, why doesn't she come in a train yaar" now Abhi was speaking by holding nose with one hand.

"Security, still largest population of India prefers Bus service than Train because they feel it more secure than trains" I poured some drops of knowledge from my brain compartment in front of Abhi but he held his nose more tightly.

Priya's bus came and I saw Priya coming down from bus holding a bag in hand. Abhi shouted to call her by letting go of his nose for a while.

She noticed us and a beautiful smile occupied her face. Despite the journey of bus she was still looking fresh. Her facial expressions seemed to be changed like a mature lady but her innocent smile was still the same. Definitely she had changed little bit but she was still our beautiful Priya.

She came towards us and greeted both of us with hugs "How are you Priya, how was the journey?" I initiated with the two typical questions while Abhi turned to pick up the bag.

"I am fine Mit. Tell me how are you?"

"As in front of you, nothing else" we started walking towards rickshaw stand with normal conversation.

"Where do we going first?" Priya asked while sitting in the rickshaw.

"Very first, at my home mom is eagerly waiting for you, there you will become fresh and we will have a lunch together over there and at evening a nice hang out" I revealed all days plan in front of her.

"Oh you have planned everything" Priya surprised.

Oh let me tell you one thing, my mom is a big fan of Priya. She loves her a lot. When she heard that she was coming after a long holiday at home she insisted on bringing her home for lunch. What luck yaar, my mom likes the same girl Dhanu's mom hates, what if Dhanu's mom could think like my mom, but I know it's not possible at all.

We reached at home and after a beautiful lunch Abhi and me sat in a hall watching TV while Priya and mom were busy in there typical female chat in kitchen.

"Hey dude what's going on over there?" Abhi asked curiously

"How could I know yaar, leave them. Let's take a snap" I stretched legs on sofa and prepared myself for sleep, Abhi laid himself on a bed.

"Mit beta wake up, did you want to miss your train today?" mom's voice struck my ears and my eyes opened in response "Oh shit, its five thirty." I woke up immediately after watching a clock, "mom wake this donkey also I am getting fresh" I moved towards bathroom. I saw Priya was making tea in the kitchen 'Oh what a fool Dhanu is he doesn't know what he has missed in life and when he will realize it, it will be too late' I mumbled to myself and moved ahead.

We left home at six I took my luggage with me to go directly from station, I said goodbye to mom and left the home, we reached at CCD to have a coffee moreover, to have a chat.

We managed to sit near a glass window where the flowing road can be seen.

"Hey, What were you talking about to Mit's mom for hours?" Abhi bounced a query soon after landing.

Priya took a pause and answered while looking at the table "I told her everything"

"Everything?" Abhi wondered

"Yes, I told her about my pregnancy. I told her about Dhanu" She was still looking at the table, but this answer was not as shocking for me as Abhi, because I know Priya needed some female support to share her problem, we are her friends but we are after all boys we can never give that kind of support and love that she needed this time from a mother, and I know my mom, she is damn good at this side.

"Okay, leave this yaar. It's fine, Priya tell me now what you have decided, I mean just tell me what your mind says" I asked her directly.

"I thought a lot on this Mit, and after talking with your mom I have decided to abort, I am ready to abort this child. I want to start a new life, I want to forget everything, I don't want to blame somebody for his mistake my whole life. I want to move ahead my friends, I want to move" Priya burst into tears and Abhi took her head on his shoulders to calm her, there was complete silence for couple of minutes only Priya's weeping could be heard.

I was speechless, I couldn't just find the words to start with. I could see Abhi's eyes asking me to say something to console Priya, but friends really, I was feeling like an immature fourth standard boy, who couldn't justify her decision nor even protest it, the only thing I can do was that I could agree with everything she had decided, we can be a strong force behind her decisions, we can be her best buddies at this point of life.

"Hey, Priya is this a time to cry beta? You have started a new life yaar, leave everything behind. You know I have heard somewhere a very great thought which I will never forget at any moment of my life 'Never cry for a relation, because the one for whom you are crying doesn't deserve your tears and the one who deserves your tears will never let you cry' so just chill out Priya start a new life" and I did my job Abhi gave me a thumbs up to congratulate me on a job well done.

"Thanks Mit and Abhi you both are real gems of my life, now tell me what to order, this is my treat okay?" said Priya taking charge now.

"Okay baba, order whatever you want. We want coffee only" said Abhi.

It was nice to see her happy again after a long time, I know this happiness was just to show us that she was happy with us, but being betrayed in real love is a kind of wound which is very difficult to heal as time passes it becomes more deep and painful.

We reached the station on time, and the train was ready to depart. I found my seat, managed to place the luggage and came immediately at the door "Hey Mit take care of yourself and don't forget to call me when you reach Ahmedabad" Priya said and I nodded.

It was an emotional moment that I will never forget and it was the last time when I met them both. After that this phone call …marriage? They are marrying each other and here I know nothing yaar, how's that possible….. something is there, something that they have not discussed yet with me. Anyways they will tell me everything but my mind it's still not accepting it as a reality yaar..kya karu I never had thought about them like this…anyways this is life. There is always a beautiful morning after a dark and scary night, so have some patience Mr. Mit.

15
IN MUMBAI: UNRAVELING THE MYSTERY

I opened my eyes. it's a nice morning my body started feeling humidity of environment a drop of sweat rolled behind my ears and I realized that I had reached Mumbai, It's always a nice feeling when you reach your hometown after a long time, you feel like the whole town is your home and you are back at home, I feel the same every time I reach Mumbai.

I crossed the sky walk of the station and found Abhi standing with hands folded and smiling at me.

I couldn't stop myself from smiling in response, and hugged him "How are you, you devil?"

"Bloody fool, I traveled the whole night standing in General compartment I didn't sleep at all, you frightened me in such a manner that I couldn't wait for reservations. I just managed to come somehow on the next train, and now you are giving a smile and asking just how are you?" I spluttered.

"Relax Mr. Mit you will get to know everything, first come with me"

"Tell me first where Priya is and where are you taking me?"

"She is at your home with your mom and I am taking you to the same place"

"What? That means mom also knows everything and she also didn't tell me" I become more frustrated.

Abhi was calm and just delivering a series of mysterious smiles, oh god! I became more frustrated.

We reached at my sweet home. Mom and Priya were at the door waiting for me with bigger smile on their faces. Oh! Finally this journey ended in good moment, let's see what's further.

My tense face become calm after seeing their smiling faces and I entered the home happily, after all typical welcomes and greetings mom brought a cup of coffee and we sat in the hall, mom and Priya sat in front of me Abhi and me were on the sofa.

"Hey, please tell me fast, are you serious or you all are just kidding with me" I asked with the same curiosity while lifting up the cup of coffee.

"This all is absolutely true Mit, are we that mad to call you so urgently from Ahmedabad" Abhi replied teasingly.

"Oh, great if it is really true then I am the happiest person, congrats yaar" I stood up with great enthu and All the worry, all the tension disappeared suddenly from my face and I hugged Abhi.

"Thanks Mit, I knew you will definitely support our decision" Abhi became senti, its really nice to see new improved version of Abhi.

"Hey what is support yaar I am always with you, and I am glad for Priya I know you will keep her always happy" I replied while looking at Priya's face, she was happy and definitely she was looking comfortable with her decision.

"Hey, now leave everything and tell me how all this happened yaar, I am dying to know the story yaar" I expressed my eagerness.

"Relax Mr. Mit, I will tell you the whole story" Abhi kept his cup aside and turned towards me.

"Do you remember Mit that night me and Priya came to drop you at railway station"

"Yeah, definitely yaar"

"Okay, kids give me permission. I have to go to market. Today Priya will cook for all of us so there is a lots of preparation to do, you carry on with your story, bye" Mom interrupted as she got a good reason to give us privacy, that's why I love my mom, she is cute.

"Wait mom, I am coming I have to do some shopping" Priya stood up to company mom.

"Bye mom, bye Priya" we both replied in one voice, its good mom and Priya left the place at right time now we can talk more freely, I turned to Abhi to ask what's next and he started immediately.

"After Railway station we went to our kaatta, and sat there almost for an hour, Priya was silent and I was just feeling helpless, first time in the life I was helpless I was incapable of wiping her tears, I was speechless. I did not know how to share her pain. We both were silent and that time I missed you a lot my friend, I thought I must do something to make her happy and asked her to come somewhere for dinner, Priya broke her silence and said 'Take me somewhere where no one would disturb us and where we can drink'

I was shocked, this is a girl who always instructed me to stay away from alcohol, who never touched alcohol in her life and nor anyone from her family but I could feel her condition, I thought it's the only way to reduce her pain to make her happy at least for a moment and I decided to take her for a drink I started my bike, bought a bottle of Bacardi white and some cold drinks and we reached at my room. That's the only safe place I knew.

Me and priya went to the terrace. I managed everything, my CD player, a CD of Enrique's collection , a mat to relax, glasses and all, I was just honestly trying to make the moments enjoyable for her.

That was a full moon night, and a magnificent, star studded sky was spreading his beautiful breezy light all over and definitely she was looking awesome in moonlight, Priya and I relaxed on the mat by leaning our backs to the wall of terrace.

"Do you still miss him Priya?" I asked her.

"Yes and I think it will be very difficult for me to forget and forgive him" Priya said, staring into space. I realized she is just physically present here.

I silently made two pegs. I was finding myself incapable of consoling her so I chose to stay silent and offered her a peg.

She took it, I turned the CD player on and Enrique's beautiful song started to make the moment more magical the song was "Miss you" we relaxed and took a sip.

After two sips I got the confidence I was lacking and I turned my face towards her "Priya, can I tell you something?"

"Yeah"

"How long?For how long Priya? For how long are you going to entertain your pain, are you going to let people blame you and your true love for the sake of that bloody monkey who never understood you and your true love. I know it's difficult to forget, but it's not impossible to forget a black chapter of life specially when you have more loving and caring people around you" it feels nice when you motivate someone and it starts working , Priya was looking at me and I could see her facial expressions changing.

"You are right Abhi, I have more loving and caring people, I have my parents who trust me, I have Mit, I have you. I promise you Abhi I will change, I will leave my past behind and from tomorrow morning you will see a new Priya" she smiled. Oh god! I made her smile finally.

"That's the spirit yaar, and I think that is not the effect of spirit" I mocked and lift a glass for cheers.

Glasses clashed and made a beautiful sound, and we decided to make it a sound of new beginning a happy beginning.

We finished two pegs and environment become little bit light, she left every sorrow behind and we were talking on different subjects, like comedy scenes from movies some funny moments of life, she was happy and I was satisfied. I was looking at her smiling face. She was looking awesome in the moon light, I could really die at the moment.

She took a glass from my hand and kept it aside "Now enough Abhi, we should stop drinking now"

"Okay, as you wish" I relaxed more against the wall and she kept her head on my shoulders, you can't imagine what happened inside me, I was feeling lighter than the air. Oh god! stop the time here, I can carry her on my shoulders for my whole life, but the next moment I felt I am being selfish, I have to control my emotions, she trusts me and I can never think for her like this yaar.

I made her lie down on the mat slowly and stood up, she was feeling sleepy but I had to drop her at her room anyhow.

"Priya wake up, we have to go to your room, come on" I tried to make her conscious, she slowly opened her eyes and glared at me for a moment.

"I don't think I can, Abhi. Let me sleep here please" she refused to wake up with a cute smile, I was killed at the spot yaar, but no Abhi you have to manage the situation, I told myself to remain strong. "No way Priya, I will not listen to you now, we have to go. Come on, you can do it, just relax and trust me, okay?" I lifted her up and held her hands to make her walk.

She came down slowly from stairs I was holding her shoulders, we came out of the bungalow and I made her stand in a corner and rushed towards bike. She was trying hard to balance her body, but couldn't stop herself from moving.

I started the bike and sat very carefully grabbing my shoulders very tightly, I was enjoying the moment of passion. Bacardi and Priya, both were making me charged up, and for the first time my inner soul felt clearly that I am in love and it's true love but the situation was bad. I can't tell her that, at least not in this condition.

I moved the accelerator roughly, bike took the speed of seventy, road was empty but my mind was not, I was thinking why I don't have eyes at the back of my head, so that I do not miss the chance of seeing her for more time but in this excitement I forgot to notice the turn coming next to me, one truck was coming from that turn and I failed to notice it, I went straight on the truck my front tire touched trucks right body and our bike was thrown away. I was not injured much but unfortunately Priya was injured she was thrown on a stony side of the road, her head started bleeding.

I stood up, my eyes were searching for Priya, I was scared, I was scared so much for Priya, Truck driver made a smart escape he didn't stop to at least see whether we were dead or alive, and why should he, this is bloody my mistake I was running the bike on seventy at the turn.

I reached Priya, she was unconscious, her head was bleeding. I took my napkin and tied her head with that tightly to stop it bleeding.

I was scared, what to do in this situation, my hand went to my pocket to search for my mobile and fortunately it was there, I immediately dialed Gulab's number, he was at his friend's room for preparations, I told him to come immediately with a car. I knew he can manage it and my bike had become useless, I took Priya's head on my laps and stared at her calm face, tears rolled down from my eyes, I was crying for the first time in my life. If anything had happened to her I would have never forgiven myself, I would be the only culprit.

Gulab came there in ten minutes. We took Priya to the city hospital. we rushed so hard it was one thirty of the night, Doctors rushed and took her immediately to the ICU, doctors requested me to come for dressing as my injuries were also bleeding but I refused, I refused to leave her alone, I said I will never leave her alone specially when she needs me a lot, I used to stand outside the ICU for whole night, Gulab also remained there, for the first time he saw me frustrated in such a manner.

At morning 5:00 Doctor came to me and took my hand "Hello Mr. Patil I am Dr. sheikh"

"Hello sir, How is Priya now" I asked him eagerly

"she is Totally out of danger now Mr. Patil, but very sorry to say that we couldn't save her child, she got miscarriage, I am sorry Mr. Patil but this is the life some compromises are always there with happiness, but I know you will handle the situation you are really a caring husband" Doctor was giving me condolence but I was totally shocked to react, I couldn't even see at his face, he left the place and Gulab came to me, sat near me and hugged "Hey, don't worry tiger, everything will be all right we will talk to Priya, she will understand"

I couldn't stop myself crying, I was collapsed totally I needed a shoulder to cry "Hey, Abhi chill yaar and I am sorry I told doctor that you both are husband wife, actually I was having no choice he was enquiring me I thought it will be safe" Gulab was telling innocently, and smile came upon my face.

"you devil you will never change" I mocked him and wiped my tears.

"Hey, wait I will bring a cup of tea" Gulab rushed to bring a tea.

A hot steamy cup of tea came and I relaxed a little bit, "Hey, Abhi don't you think that we should call her parents" Gulab asked while taking a sip.

"Yeah, I was thinking of that only, but what to tell them yaar, what will they feel about Priya that their daughter was drunk and riding on a bike at midnight with a boy, and a height upon all this she was pregnant! Bloody bullshit yaar, I can't" I expressed my frustration.

"No way yaar, just leave it upto me I will handle all this, they are her parents they should be here with her and nothing will happen even if they knows at this stage believe me they are going to know it some day then why not now buddy" Gulab gave me confidence that everything will be fine, my mind was confused to understand what he is saying and what he is going to do but gave him permission to do whatever he wish because I was only worried for Priya I needed to be there with her.

"Sir, you can meet your patient" a nurse came from ICU to inform us, I stood up to go there, "Abhi you go in I will call her parents" Gulab took my permission to go, and I went to Priya.

I wiped my eyes and went near her bed, her head was covered with the band aid, her eyes were closed and still I can feel calmness on her face, I sat on a chair near her bed, she opened her eyes glared me and smiled "Are you okay Abhi".

"Absolutely, I am fine .... I am so sorry Priya all this happened just because of me" my eyes become moist.

"Hey, Abhi don't think like this, its okay" she hold my hand, and I become more emotional.

"I think you are not slept whole night" said Priya

"hmm.. I was just worried for you" I took hanky to wipe out eyes.

"Nurse told me about my baby" said Priya glaring outside of window.

"You knew it Priya?" I was surprised as this is the most threatening news I was scared to tell her but she knows it and she didn't reacted at all.

"Yes, as soon as I listened it I was depressed a lot but later on I thought I never deserved that child, I never cared for him, I was just thinking about my self I was being selfish all the time, so, I lost him and that's the destiny" Priya was talking so silently and calmly and all her words were hurting me deeply.

"I am sorry Priya"

"Don't be, its okay, last night a new Priya is borne, all the previous tensions and problem got vanished, and I am going to live a new life, I learned to know peoples Abhi, and I am lucky that I have friends like you and mit" a cute smile came again on her face and I realized that its really a new start. So, buck up Abhi be a winner.

"Okay, thanks Priya, umm.. another thing Gulab is calling your parents we thought they should be with you at this moment" I told her innocently and waited for reaction.

"thanks, actually I was gonna tell you the same, I am missing my mom Abhi and I knows my mom and dad well they will understand the situation" Oh!... what a great relief she took away all my worries.

"Mr. Patil Doctor is calling you" a nurse informed me from the door of ICU.

"I will just come Priya"

"Okay"

I took her permission and left the place, I was feeling some kind of change from inner side I was behaving like a responsible husband I don't know, what is this and how is this but I was feeling really good from inner side.

"yeah, come on Mr. Patil, please have a chair" Doctor welcomed me as he saw me at the door.

"Actually I am not having much time but I just wanna have some words with you"

"yeah, please sir" I was eager to listen what he is saying.

"Mr. Patil, I am really glad to see such a caring husband like you" Doctor initiated a conversation.

I chuckled and said "thanks for the compliment sir"

"No no, no thanks Mr. Patil its true, I invited you here just to tell you something, I know its very painful to came to know that your first child is no more which hasn't seen the life yet, and more painful is to see a loving wife in ICU, but you have to be more careful about her I am going to tell you one more shocking news and I hope you will take it sportingly"

"what sir?" I really become impatient like a husband, and started to feel myself as a what doctor is feeling.

"Mr. Patil your wife can never be a mother again, we had taken that step just to save her I know its painful but its just to save her life" Doctor finished him and waited for the reaction but I become introword I become speechless, I was thinking only about Priya how to tell it to her can she bear one more shock, no way I will not let her know it at least not now.

"Doctor its okay, its really a destiny, but please you have to consider my one request"

"Yeah, tell me"

"please don't tell this to Priya"

"Okay, Mr. Patil as you wish, it will be between you and me only"

"one more thing sir Priya's parents will come today, please don't tell it to them also"

"You don't worry Mr. Patil, I am a professional person" Doctor reassured me, I took a long breath and stood up to left his cabin.

"Thank you so much sir"

"Its my pleasure Mr. Patil"

As I came towards the ICU I saw Gulab coming towards me "What happen Gulab"

"Nothing yaar, I informed to her parents they will come at any time , and one thing we have to pay some advance"

"Okay, how much?"

"five thousand, did you have it?"

"yeah, I have to check"

"Look Abhi, I have these two thousands, keep it you will need it" Gulab offered some rupees from his pocket.

"Thanks yaar" I took it and he hugged me with love.

"Okay listen, now go to room have a bath then bring some food for three of us, I will be here with Priya" Gulab instructed as a father.

"Okay, I need to be fresh, Priya is taking a rest I will come from room, bye" I started to walk away from him, after walking some distance Gulab called me "Hey, Abhi listen" I stopped and turned he rushed towards me.

"Hey, Abhi did you love her?" Gulab asked looking into my eyes.

"have you gone mad Gulab" I tried to avoid answering.

"Hey, tell me seriously, did you?"

"no way yaar" I moved back and started to walk but after some distance my legs stopped to walk and I turned towards Gulab.

"Hey Gulab, I think yes" I yelled from hospital gate and Gulab jumped in joy.

16
MEETING MOM AND DAD

I went to my room, first took nap to get rid of the dizzy, drowsy feeling, and after an hour I took a bath and purchased some food from kaki's canteen and marched again to hospital. As I reached the hospital gate I saw gulab at the corridor as soon as he noticed me, he rushed to me "Hey, Abhi listen come here" Gulab pulled me into a corner.

"Hey, what happened?" I spluttered

He put his hand on my mouth to tell me to keep quiet and said "Yaar Priya's mom and dad are here"

My heart started beating fast "Then, where are they?"

"Mom is in the ICU talking with Priya, and dad is with Dr. sheikh in his cabin"

"Okay, did they ask you anything?" I started enquiring just to get the idea of the situation.

"Umm.. just about accident, not much yaar, actually they spoke with the Priya more and dad went to meet Dr. sheikh" Gulab answered like a witness of a case.

"okay, you stay here. I will go to Dr. sheikh's cabin" I rushed towards doctors cabin. As soon as I reached there, my feet stopped. I took a pause before entering the door, I heard Dr. Sheikh's voice.

" My condolences are with you Dr. Joshi but you should be thankful to the almighty god that you have got such a good son in law. He is such a caring husband, your daughter is really lucky Dr.Joshi"

Oh god, how can I commit such a silly mistake?, I forgot to tell Dr. Sheikh about this fake husband tragedy, shit everything is finished, now I can't face Priya's Father. Mr. Patil now you are fucked up you started to think yourself as a real hubby and your day dreaming has now kicked your ass.

I left the place immediately, without entering in the cabin and dragged Gulab with me who was waiting for me in the corridor.

"Hey, dude what happened where you taking me?"

"I need a ciggy" I muttered.

We reached at café outside the hospital. I took a cigarette lightened it and took a puff.

"Now tell me what happened?" Gulab asked curiously.

"Yaar, Dr. Sheikh told Priya's father everything"

"Everything? What?"

"Everything means everything you fool, he told him that I am his daughter's husband, and we lost our child in the accident" I spluttered.

"What? Then how did he react?"

"I don't know"

"Oh, shit yaar it's a mess"

Gulab blazed one more ciggy to join me. Few minutes passed and Mr. Gulab started to pass condolences to me.

"Hey Abhi don't get tensed yaar, I know Priya will handle the situation, because as a father he will first ask Priya about this and Priya will definitely handle the dilemma. So nothing will come directly to you yaar"

"It's not about me yaar, how a father will feel after knowing that his only daughter has a boyfriend not only a boyfriend but she is also pregnant and they came to know only when she met an accident at late night and lost her child. It's ridiculous yaar. I don't know how Dr. Joshi will react on this" I expressed my depression and took one more deep puff.

"But do you think we will get a reward for sitting here and cursing ourselves at this crucial time at least you should be there yaar, face them and answer them, my tiger!" Gulab was trying to encourage me, but it's very hard to get motivated when you have to take part in swimming competition and only you know that you aren't wearing innerwear.

But it's Okay Mr. Abhi you have to be there I instructed myself and stood up to go.

"Best of luck buddy" Gulab raised his hands to wish me good luck.

I went to the ICU. Priya's parents were sitting beside her and seemed to be busy in talking about some serious issue, I just went there and stood at some distance, where Priya can notice me.

"Papa, this is Abhi" Priya pointed a finger towards me and I tried to present myself as a descent guy.

"Oh! Youngman you are Abhi, please come beta" Priya's father welcomed me as a family member and gave me a hug.

What's happening yaar? It's a miracle! I was expecting something completely different.

"Sir, I have brought some food, please take it" I offered a bag of Tiffin to them.

"So nice of you beta. Did you have your lunch?" Mrs. Joshi asked me very caringly.

"Yes aunty, this is for you" I tried to be more descent.

"Okay ladies you carry on with your chatting. I will take a walk with Abhi, come on beta" Dr. Joshi signaled me to follow him and I had no choice.

Dr. Joshi stopped at canteen outside hospital and turned to me "Abhi let's have a cup of tea"

166

"Yeah sure sir" I replied formally and I could guess what was going to happen in the next few minutes.

I ordered two cups of tea. Dr. Joshi relaxed in the chair "So Mr. Abhishek, I can guess my only daughter is really very impressed by you, she can't stop talking about you"

"It's just her nature sir there's nothing great about me" I replied with somewhat 'Amol Palekar' type of expressions on my face.

"No Abhishek, I am also impressed by you, you are really a responsible and caring guy I think my daughter has made the right choice"

My mouth remained practically open on hearing the words of 'Shri Shri Param pujya Dr. Joshi', the first and only person bearing so novel thoughts about me.

"I got to know everything from Dr. Sheikh, beta I am not that kind of person who always loves to make issue of everything, I know my daughter's real happiness and where it lies and I trust her, if she commits any mistake she has guts to repair it, so tell me when are you people going to marry" Uncle asked direct question on which I am speechless because situation is really different.

"Sir I think I should talk with Priya first and then we both will answer you" I tried to patch up the situation.

"Okay, nice beta take your decision but keep it in mind I wanted to fix your marriage as early as possible. I will talk to your father you don't worry about that"

"Okay sir fine" the subject ended and my mind started to find a time to talk with Priya. It really necessary to tell her the dilemma and I was really worried that how will she react, Uff...what a mess yaar when I was thinking that Priya's father will hate me that was a problem for me but now when he likes me that's another problem for me. Fine Mr. Abhi you have to face it.

After some time Mr. and Mrs. Joshi went to the canteen to have lunch and I got the golden moment to have a chat with Priya.

I reached the ICU, Priya was lying on the bed with her eyes closed, but seemed to be thinking something very hard in her mind.

"Are you really feeling sleepy or just trying to look like that" I asked something to notify my presence.

"Oh, Abhi! I was just thinking of you" Priya greeted me with a decent smile.

"So, How was the reaction?"

"Quite okay, I knew that they will not overreact like filmy mom and dad but.." Priya took a pause suddenly staring in the infinity.

"But what?"

"There is some misunderstanding Abhi, they are assuming us to be a couple" Priya answered with a low voice.

"And then did you explain to them what is really happening?"

Priya looked nervous like a scandalous person who finds himself shameful in accepting his crime "No Abhi I couldn't, actually I don't want to give them one more shock. They are already suffering from lots of pain just because of me, and now if they comes to know that the father of my dead child is someone else who has already dumped me after making me pregnant, they will definitely break down"

Priya's eyes become moist. She broke down into tears and I took her into my arms "Oh, don't cry Priya now nothing is going to be wrong into your life now no one is going to ditch you or no one will ever hurt you"

I looked into Priya's eyes they were full of emotions, hope and life I realized that this is the perfect time and I said those magical words "Priya I love you, I love you so much. I don't know when, how I fell in love with you but I promise that I will never leave you alone. I will always be with you in the morning, in afternoon, in evening, in the night, midnight every day of the week, every week of the month, every month of an year, in sad times, in happy moments, in worries, in relief; I will be there with you in each and every second of your life Priya trust me I will make you the happiest girl of the world"

I poured my heart in front of her, she was still looking into my eyes she seemed to be so shocked that she couldn't speak a word for a while, I released her from my hug. A silence occupied the space between us and after some time I realized that I did something wrong and moved to wake up.

"Wait Abhi, you said everything you want to say and what about me can I say something to you?"

"Yeah" I replied and prepared myself for listening to her 'No'.

"Abhi I know you are a good person, better friend and the best husband. You took care of me like I am a baby, it was only you who was always with me in my bad times, you have never left me alone, you are the only person I can trust, I can share my feelings freely with you, you are my best buddy but…." Priya made a pause which was making a hole in my heart.

"But.. I know what is next to this 'but' Priya, leave it. I can understand your problems" I stood up and walked towards the door.

"But I don't want to trouble you more Abhi, I don't want you to be stuck with me for a life time" Priya continued and ended by making me more upset, I turned back to her, get closer to her and cupped her face "Did you still think I am doing all this just for the sake of sympathy for a friend, you were always wrong about me Priya, because you never noticed my love for you, you took all my concern for granted, you never looked at me from any another angle, all I did to bring you and Dhanu closer was just to make you happy, to give you all you wanted, but that silly fellow ditched you. I didn't recognize him, believe me all I want in my life is just to see you happy that's all, and I love you from the moment I saw you for the first time and will continue loving you till last moment of life" I was looking into her eyes and she was speechless. I got my face closer to her and kissed on her lips.

"huu…husband and wife seemed to be very busy" someone coughed from ICU cabins door to make us aware of his presence, we immediately separated and maintained distance to look normal and I looked back it was Dr. sheikh.

"Oh, sir please come we were just chatting" I replied.

"yeah, I know it's okay young man I also love my wife very much and you know even at this stage of our marital life, she never forgets to give me a goodnight and goodbye kiss. It's very important in life to make your partner to feel your love and affection for him, otherwise life makes us so busy that we forget about each other's feelings" Dr. sheikh seemed to be remembering his young days.

"Okay, how is my patient feeling now, I think time has come to move you out of ICU" Dr. sheikh started his general checkup .

"No, doctor time has come to move your patient out of the hospital, she is getting married soon and your hospital is a turning point of her second life" Priya's father entered the room.

"Oh! That means these children's are yet not bounded by a knot of marriage, then what you all are waiting for? Don't be too late Dr. Joshi, you will not get such a good son-in-law" Dr. sheikh admired me and I honestly tried to feel shy.

"you will soon get the marriage card Doctor" Dr. Joshi assured

"Okay, give me a permission, and I will discharge your daughter very soon" Dr. sheikh left the hall

"Yes, Abhi can I talk to your father, I think we should try to arrange everything in this month only" Priya's father asked.

I know next step will be definitely calling my father and Pre marital discussions of elders but my boat of love is still finding a way in

Priya's river of heart. I was unable to say anything without Priya's signal. Oh! God what a mess! I looked at Priya to find out an answer to her father's question, and at that moment god listened to my prayers. That was a golden moment for me Priya held my hand and blinked her eyes in affirmative way.

Uff! Here's everything I wanted I felt like riding on ninth cloud I immediately said "Yes sir I will call my father here by tomorrow, you can talk to him about marriage preparations".

I left the place in a very glad mood as everything was going the right way. I came out of the hospital and sat on the bike to start it but suddenly, I stopped myself. Something stirred my mind instantly.

I hadn't talked to my father about all this and I was assuming his agreement, but I assured myself that I will convince him. I knew my father was a little bit orthodox but he could compromise at one point for his only child's happiness, Love marriage was totally new stuff for our family and inter cast marriage! Oh god! Please help again.

I reached my room, parked my bike near the room and opened the gate as usual, suddenly I paused in shock. My father's car was parked in the front yard. Oops! I didn't know what to think, whether everything was still going the right way or was this the start of a new twist in my life.

In the same confused state, I pressed the door bell. The door was opened by Gulab his facial expression was just like a person who has recently seen a major accident and his voice came out like a warning bell "Your father has came"

I nodded and proceeded in the room,my father was sitting in front of the TV watching news "Hi, baba, how are you?" I greeted him with expressionless face.

"Oh! My son, come here" he stood up and hugged me with love.

It was really senti moment for me but my mind was busy in getting ready for another tragic moment planted in the future.

"It's a great surprise baba, how did you come suddenly?" I enquired gathering words with effort.

"Nothing my son, I had a business meeting in Mumbai, so I also planned to meet you, first of all you get ready we will have a lunch together your mother has sent some food for you".

I went to the bathroom and Gulab caught me in the way "Hey what happened? Did you propose her?" Gulab asked curiously.

I couldn't collect words to answer him at the moment so I smiled at him and shook my head and this signal was enough to tell him everything is okay, he jumped with the joy and hugged me "Now what's next buddy, how will you handle baba?"

"Let's pray for good" I moved to get fresh.

17
A BIG CONFESSION

There was a pin drop silence in the room. Baba was busy in eating paratha's and alu sabji from his plate and reading messages on his mobile. I was busy in playing with the same stuff called paratha's in my plate and Gulab was busy in observing us silently.

"Would you like to take one more paratha Abhi" Gulab asked to attract my attention.

I looked at him and he made a big question mark on his face, I understood and signaled him to remain silent.

"Baba, Abhi wants to tell you something important", Gulab now turned his march towards baba to ignite me.

"Yeah, Abhi what happened?" Baba became curious to know, what his only son was hesitating in telling him.

"Baba, actually it is a very big thing. I should have told you earlier but everything just happened suddenly and I didn't get the time to talk with you, please don't misunderstand" I initiated somehow.

"No way son, tell me I will help you if there is any problem" baba assured me.

"Umm.. Baba I love a girl and her parents wish to talk to you" I revealed the core secret directly.

Baba kept the piece of paratha in the plate which was about to enter into his mouth, it was a serious discussion for him so he wanted to concentrate totally on me not on the paratha's.

"It's ok, my son, even I was thinking about asking you whether you like any girl or not, so tell me what's her name and what her father does" I heaved a sigh hearing first reaction of baba, but I know my father the main panic is further, he asked name to know the cast and I have no choice, I can't hide for a long time from my father that I wanted to marry a Brahmin girl.

"Baba her name is Priya ..... Priya Joshi and her parents are doctor" I muttered avoiding eye contact.

"Joshi? That means girl is from Brahmin family and parents are doctor which tells that she is from good background" Baba started his analysis.

"Yeah Baba they have their clinic in Pune" I disturbed his analytical process as I become more excited and eager to listen his yes.

"And we are Maratha's , I guess her parents do not have any problem about the inter cast marriage right?" Baba obstructed me and asked the core question.

"yeah they don't believe in the castes and they want to meet you to know your view first" now I become calm after knowing that there is still a long way to travel.

"Yeah, world has gone very far and we people are still digging ourselves in the castism, I think I should meet them son you can call them in the morning, let's see what is my son's choice is" Baba finished his dinner and moved to bedroom Gulab and me were still busy in our plates.

As soon as lights of Baba's room got off Gulab jumped from his chair 'Hey Abhi, congrats man you have won the half battle'

Yes it was really like that as these reactions are totally unexpected from Baba. we have seen him as an orthodox man and who always stuck to the traditional values but his this avatar was surprising for us. May be parents really change with the age of their child and also they really tries to adopt themselves with the new generation mind of their children's, I thanked god for that night and prayed for the blessed morning.

Next morning Priya's Mom and Dad arrived at my house around eleven, about one hour after I called them, I had the same feeling one has just before reading a question paper of tough subject while sitting in the exam hall.

It was really an exam day for me Dr. Joshi's car stopped in front of my house and butterflies started to flutter in my tummy.

I went to the door to greet them, Baba was busy reading newspaper, I welcomed Mr. and Mrs. Joshi in the room and Baba kept the newspaper aside to greet them and his face sparked after seeing at Dr. Joshi.

"Oh! Joshya it's you? I am surprised what a destiny; we both are meeting in this manner"

"Yes after about thirty years of gap"

'Come in yaar, let's have a hug, Joshya, my son wants to marry your daughter! Do you have any problem?"

"What are you asking yaar? If I knew that Abhi is your son I would have brought a pandit with me"

I was feeling overwhelmed after being a witness of this 'mitramilan' and after that I had a very little role to play in between them they decided all the things about marriage Oh! god how kind you are to me.

Later on I got to know that Baba and Dr. Joshi were classmates in their junior college days when baba was studying in Pune. After HSC Baba took admission in law and Dr. Joshi took admission in medical college of Pune but despite that they remained roommates in Pune for four years and now they were meeting after about twenty four years, what a Destiny!

Everything was going in my and Priya's favor. I went to my room and called Priya to share this good news 'Hey, Mrs. Patil, congrats' I initiated as she picked up the phone.

"Hmmm.. it seems that his highness Abhishek sir, has won the battle"

"Obviously yaar, I am very happy, and now I am sure that it's our destiny to meet, no one can stop us now Priya, we ..are.. made for …each…other" I whispered in a romantic tone.

I told everything to Priya that how destiny was working for us, "Uff.. what an idiot I am yaar I am telling all this over phone? Then how could i see the happiness on your face" I jumped saying this and threw away my cell on bed and rushed to door.

"Hey, Abhi where are you going son?" Baba yelled.

"Baba ..urgent work I will just come" I mumbled hastily without looking back.

"Let him go Patil, stop asking him silly questions now he wants to share this news with his girlfriend" Dr. Joshi mocked me and that trio started laughing.

Now who cares yaar I kicked my bike and went to Priya's Room where Priya was staying after being discharged from the hospital. When I reached there she was busy in packing.

I knocked the slightly open door, Priya looked up curiously and an innocent smile appeared on cute face, a bunch of some rebel curly hairs were touching her lips beautifully and I froze there only.

"What happened Mr. Patil? Getting romantic? But you have to wait for some time" she joked with a killing smile.

"Yeah ma'm, I know and this 'ghulam' is ready to wait a whole life for you"

"Now don't make me senti ha, come on, help me in packing"

"For whom you are packing sweetie? Our parents have decided to tie our knot on coming Sunday and you and your parents will stay in our bungalow only"

"You mean this Sunday?" Priya surprised

"Yes baba this Sunday, any problem?"

"It's a very little time Abhi how could I get a time for my marriage shopping?"

"Don't worry beta, I am here to help. I will assist you and baba will assist Dr. Joshi for marriage preparations" I reveled my plan by sitting beside her

"Don't call him Dr. Joshi ha"

"Then what should I call him ma'm" I asked softly getting closer to her

"Call him papa" she whispered in my ears.

"Ok, no problem and what should I call you? ….Pappi?" I bantered and Priya and I busted into a laugh enjoying magical moments of our life.

18
THE BIGGEST DAY

"Hushhh... so my friend this is the whole story of our marriage" Abhi completed his narration with a big sigh at the end.

"And believe me...... in all this I couldn't get the time to inform you, but my friend I knew that ultimately you will be the happiest man at the end."

"Off course Abhi I am the happiest man" I hugged him with face full of smile.

So, things are going through right track finally. And this story is very near to its happy ending, my friends are going to fulfill each other's life's with Love, care and lots of Joy and I know this gonna be a perfect couple as both knows each other's plus and minus points very well so, there never will be a place for any type of misunderstanding or disbelief in there relation and I am damn sure this is a happy ending of all sad times through which Priya and Abhi has suffered.

'Hey, Devil what are you thinking so seriously yaar come on there are only three days for marriage we have to do lots of preparations' Abhi called me while wearing sox to go out.

'Yeah, am coming buddy' I yelled in response.

Three days passed very rapidly and the marriage day came, in these three day's we did only three things shopping, shopping and lots of shopping! When you are sharing a joy with your near and dear ones time always matters least.

I was busy wearing a shirt and staring at my smiling face in mirror my phone rang I saw it was a unknown number I picked it " Halo Mit" voice came from other side.

"yeah, who's it"

"Hi, it's Dhanu remember my friend?"

I was just shocked to listen these words from other side, 'Dhanu?' He was never expected by me at this moment how can this bastard call me at this time and what should I talk to him.

"How are you Mit?" He continued.

"Yeah, speak up fast is there anything urgent?" I replied in a rude way.

"No, nothing my friend I just wanted to wish Priya and Abhi for their married life"

"Oh then, you know about the marriage, then why don't you wish yourself"

"I know they will not talk to me"

"Okay I am in a hurry, we will talk some other time" I cut the phone because I didn't want to disturb my mind with his foolish talk, I threw the cell phone and diverted my mind to get ready for marriage.

"It was really nice function how you boy's arranged everything in such a short period?" Mom couldn't stop herself from talking continuously about the wedding ceremony, it was eight in the evening and we were returning home.

"Yeah, really nice mom"

"And you noticed that? Priya was looking so cute in marriage sari just like a doll" Mom's mind was still in the marriage ceremony she was excitedly talking about the function and why should not she? after all marriage was really arranged in a nice way and bride and groom both were looking magnificent that night.

But my mind is busy in thinking something else, I was thinking of Dhanu after all he was also my friend and it's true that I can't forget him though I was busy in arranging this function. I was missing something, I was feeling incomplete from inside.

I spent that night sleepless and next morning I couldn't stop myself from going to Dhanu's home, I reached outside Dhanu's home and I realized a kind of silence which I never felt there, door was half open but curtain was hiding inner scene.

"Dhanu…" I called,without trying to open the curtain.

And one 22 – 23 years old lady came out she was wearing a simple sari her hairs were loose and wet indicating she had just taken a bath and wheat flour stuck to her hands was indicating that she is busy in some housework.

"Is Dhanu there?" I asked her humbly.

"No, he is not at home right now" answer came in a quite, nice voice.

"And uncle – aunty"

"Both have gone to the temple"

"Ok fine" I moved back immediately to go.

"Excuse me? What should I tell him?" she asked me humbly.

"Tell him Mit wants to meet you, today in the evening!" I answered without looking back.

That evening Dhanu called me and he invited me to Anna's Dhaba, I was curious to see Anna's Dhaba after such a long time.

I reached there at 7:30 and really I was surprised to see nice changes there, just like at the entrance now there was a watch man standing instructing peoples for parking their vehicles as well as saluting everyone coming in. He was earning some tips through that salute.

Anna's counter and seat had also changed and one can see now god's little wooden temple behind his seat, there are also one or two extra white hair in Anna's moustache but the smile was the same.

I stopped at the counter and stared at Anna and within ten second yellowish teeth's sparkled from behind of rowdy moustache "Hey, Mit my Boy after a long time"

I smiled gently in response.

"Where are you now a days?"

"I am in Ahmedabad Anna"

"Nice, meet your friend he is sitting at table 6 in corner" Anna shown a finger towards corner table and I saw Dhanu seating there.

I moved towards him it seemed that he had started already, a half bottle of rum was kept on his table from which one or two pegs were already extracted and Dhanu sat comfortably with Cigarette in one hand and glass in other which was indicating for sure that he was a regular visitor of this place.

"May I join you?" I asked pulling back chair to seat.

"Oh Mit! Please sit yaar, did you think that you need permission?"

"How are you my friend?" I asked something to initiate the talk.

"Oh! You called me a friend, now I am feeling well" he replied in a teasing way with blunt face.

Some seconds passed blankly, I was obsessed with initiating any topic then he said "Hey, I will make a peg for you" he poured some rum in a glass.

"No yaar Dhanu please, I quit drinking" Dhanu's hand paused suddenly and he stared at me "Oh! You might have changed your brand, change in friends and change in brand, no worry tell me which brand"

"No other brand Dhanu I don't drink and I am here just to meet you, not to have a peg"

He remained silent as my voice seemed little bit hard.

"Okay, leave it, tell me friend what's new?" I have to change the topic to make him speaking but there was no reply from his side and again couple of minutes passed away.

"Hey, morning I visited your home, mom and dad was not there but I saw a lady there, who's that" I asked curiously.

He kept his glass down and answered with the same blunt face "She is my wife" he answered without moving a single wrinkle of his face, his blunt faced was staring at me in a strange way, I got confused over this statement.

"Are you joking Dhanu?" I asked shockingly.

"I never joked Mit, it is life who always joked with me"

"When did you get married?"

"Soon after that incident"

"Why didn't you tell me?"

"Would you have attended my marriage...I know surely not"

I remained silent for a while, and he continued, "Mom fixed my marriage in very short perio,d with the daughter of one of her relatives from our village, and I was forced to marry with a less educated village girl, damn it and my life has become bullshit" he drank all the rum in the glass in one go and threw the glass in a corner with hate, the glass was broken and one waiter yelled "Dhanuanna broken one more glass" Anna wrote something in his diary and began his work.

I was surprised with this behavior of Dhanu, this was a totally different Dhanu for me. I had never thought that Dhanu would ever destroy his own life in this manner, I was speechless now, but I knew that this was the only time when I should speak up, I knew that my distracted friend needs me more when he was trying to hide his face from world.

"So, you are thinking that destiny has played a stupid joke with you, everyone around you has cheated you and you are just an innocent victim of the destiny" my voice become some more silent and serious.

"I don't know what I am thinking and what should I think, I don't know what I am doing and for what" now I was seeing a helpless and destructed Dhanu.

"Why are you thinking that a girl who married you is not of your level she is the worst thing of your life, what do you think of yourself if you are educated then you know everything haah?"

"Don't ask me more silly questions Mit please.." Dhanu sounded irritated.

"Dhanu try to understand and try to adjust with the situation around you, everything is going on just for you and your happiness, what has happened is out of your and my control, we can't change that ever, but what we can do is forget. The worse things of past and accept your present with it's purity and its real shine, remember my friend this is the only way you can live happily" I poured all my feelings at that moment.

"Yeah, I think you are right I must forget everything and live happily ..happy and calm life, it sounds so pretty nah? But how could I forget that my girlfriend married my best friend, she has married Abhi, how could I forget that?" Dhanu burst out with his frustration.

"Oh this thing is bothering you? This is the fruit of your own farm"

"No, I never made a situation like that, in spite I always had a doubt on him and he proved it right at the end"

"Do you know Dhanu what kind of nonsense you are talking?" I shouted at him.

"Yes I know very well, and listen Mit I am even suspecting now that....that child was Abhi's and they were having an affair from long time. Abhi refused to marry and they both planned to blame that child on my name" Dhanu's ridiculous talk went on, my patience was broken down and I got up from that place.

I raised my middle finger towards him and said "Go to hell Dhanu, you are a basket case and no one can entertain you now" I left the place very quickly with drastically disturbed mind, I rapidly walked at some distance from Dhaba and blazed a cigarette.

My hands were shivering, I felt like my body was releasing warm vapors, I needed some time to get calm, my eyes became wet but I know now I can't change anything. I just tried to expel that toxic talk from my mind and tried to get cool.

19
HAPPY ENDINGS (?)

After four months I traveled back to Mumbai, this city always surprises me with fast changes in it, this city is restless and every time I come to Mumbai I feel a kind of newness in it.

After meeting mom, my plan was to have a dinner with Abhi and Priya.

They invited me at their new home, and I was really more eager to meet this happily married couple than my mom.

Abhi has completed his BE and now he has joined a well known construction company in Mumbai itself, Priya has joined a computer science college as a lecturer and both were really enjoying their life together.

That night I had dinner with Abhi and Priya I was very satisfied to see their happy faces and their tuning with each other, that night after dinner we enjoyed watching their marriage CD, and a long chat at that time I really forgot about the thing called time.

And most important thing was that, Abhi remembers the Oath we took at Anna's Dhaba one day before our HSC results, The oath to change the educational system and to contribute for that he and Priya has started a learning center in slum area and they with some of volunteers teaches children's of slum area's for free, I felt so glad to hear it from Abhi and respect for Abhi is doubled in my mind.

I left their home with very fantastic mood at about 12:30 of midnight; I took a road from our college and from Anna's Dhaba to go to my home and my bike became little slow when I was passing from Anna's Dhaba, I saw Dhanu in unconscious situation, dragged by hotel waiters as Dhaba was to be closed, they laid his unconscious body on footpath and moved to close the Dhaba as it is their routine job, a tear fell from my eye but my hand moved the accelerator.